"You don't love child's dream, a dream you should have grown out of a long time ago."

"How dare you speak to me like that?" Joanna tried to pull away, but his strength was too great, a conquering strength that held her fast, his hands tightly at her waist, his eyes burning into hers.

"I will speak to you as I choose!" Nick's lips tightened. "You're *mine*, exactly what I want."

Patricia Wilson was born in Yorkshire and lived there until she married and had four children. She loves traveling and has lived in Singapore, Africa and Spain. She had always wanted to be a writer but a growing family and a career as a teacher left her with little time to pursue her interest. With the encouragement of her family, she gave up teaching in order to concentrate on writing and her other interests of music and painting.

Don't miss any of our special offers. Write to us at the following address for information on our newest releases.

Harlequin Reader Service
U.S.: 3010 Walden Ave., P.O. Box 1325, Buffalo, NY 14269
Canadian: P.O. Box 609, Fort Erie, Ont. L2A 5X3

DARK
ILLUSION
Patricia Wilson

Harlequin Books

TORONTO • NEW YORK • LONDON
AMSTERDAM • PARIS • SYDNEY • HAMBURG
STOCKHOLM • ATHENS • TOKYO • MILAN
MADRID • WARSAW • BUDAPEST • AUCKLAND

ISBN 0-373-03354-0

DARK ILLUSION

Copyright © 1992 by Patricia Wilson.

First North American Publication 1995.

CHAPTER ONE

JOANNA stared at herself in the long mirror, too numb inside to really see her own image, although this frozen disbelief was better than the sick, frightening bitterness that had been eating into her since she had known about the wedding. It would not get her through the day. Somehow she must face it, hide her feelings. Nobody knew; that was her protection. They might suspect, but if she could get through this day they would finally forget about her and Martin.

The girl who stared back at her seemed to be a stranger, the eyes no longer filled with laughter. Hair of cloudy gold hung to her shoulders, tilted eyes of jade-green and a soft, sweet mouth that was now trembling. It could hardly be her, Joanna Denton. She turned slowly, watching the dress swing with her, its cleverly cut lines accentuating her youthful figure, the slender shape, the tiny waist and high young breasts. It was her mother's taste, and Eve Calvert had perfect taste; she had selected the dress from many sent to her from London. It was the exact jade-green of Joanna's eyes.

Her hands clenched together as she moved across the room, the bitter panic threatening to resurface. She had known Martin all her life, loved him for as long as she could remember. Always it had been Joanna and Martin, the two of them inseparable. Even when she had been at college she had raced home at weekends whenever possible, simply to see him, to be with him. Nothing had ever been said, no feelings spoken aloud, but she had always known that one day she would be Martin's wife.

Well, he was getting married today, but Joanna was not the bride. She could still hear his voice when he had told her.

'I'm getting married, Jo.'

Her heart had leapt. She knew him so well, knew so easily his humour. Next he would say he had decided that she could be the bride—how else would Martin ever propose to her? They were too close for any ritual kneeling and hand-taking. She had known he was different since he had come back from London. There was an excitement about him.

He hadn't said what she had expected to hear at all, though. He had told her about Rina Martella, and the whole world had crumbled around her. That had been weeks ago, and now he was back, back for the last time. He was getting married here, at the church they had both attended as children, and the reception was here too, in her own home, but Joanna was not the bride. She was the bridesmaid.

Her mother came into the room and walked across to her, every movement a burst of nervous energy. There was little about them to denote their relationship. Joanna was taller, graceful, a slender image of her paternal grandmother, but Eve was a very sophisticated woman, a perfect foil for her busy husband, this house the background she deserved.

'Excellent!' She surveyed Joanna closely, no thought in her mind but that her daughter would look the part she had planned. 'That dress is the perfect match for your eyes.' She peered closely into Joanna's face. 'Keep your eyes wide open. I want the effect of the perfect colour-matching to be seen.' She stepped back, satisfied. 'Now get your hair up and fasten the flowers into it. They'll be here soon.'

'Flowers are for the bride.' Joanna's voice was dull, almost far away, but Eve was already briskly moving out. She saw nothing she did not want to see.

'I think she'll be covered head to foot in a veil or something.' Eve frowned slightly. 'It would have been nice to be told, actually, but as you're the only bridesmaid there'll be no chance of a clash. At least she's wearing white. I know that.'

'I don't see why she needs me as a bridesmaid,' Joanna said with a rising note of panic in her voice that she tried to control. 'After all, they're only having the reception at the manor. Surely she has friends of her own?'

'They're all in America, darling, and it's a long way. In any case, Mr Martella asked for you, and naturally Martin would want you to play a big part in his wedding, as he has no sisters. I think you're the obvious choice, and I wouldn't have been too pleased to see you left out of things as the reception is to be here. I don't intend them to outshine us.' Eve paused elegantly at the door of Joanna's room. 'Mr Martella has such influence. He wanted the wedding to be something to remember, and you can't say, Joanna, that this house is less than spectacular. We could hardly refuse when he asked. Apparently his niece wanted a very English wedding—picture-book. He's brought a good deal of business Frederick's way these last few years, and refusing this favour was out of the question. Now do hurry up and stop looking so depressed—it's not a funeral!'

She swept out and Joanna walked to the window, looking out over the grounds of Hemmington Manor. To her it was almost a funeral because it marked the death of all her hopes. In just a little while Martin would marry Rina Martella, niece of the head of the great Martella Industries, and Joanna would watch because she had no choice. She would attend the bride and see

Martin walk away married to someone else. Had Martin asked her to be the bridesmaid because Nick Martella had ordered it? Any other thought was too hurtful to contemplate. There was no cruelty in Martin.

It should have come as no surprise that her life would be ruined. She should have known by sheer instinct, because there had always been this peculiar upheaval inside her at the thought of Nick Martella. Always she had known deep down that one day he would threaten her. Since she had first seen him she had been unconsciously on guard. She even dreamed of him regularly, dark, frightening dreams that left her strangely lethargic and unsettled the next day. Even at seventeen he had alerted all her instincts, and now, six years later, it had all come to pass.

She had told herself that it was not his fault, that he was merely the girl's uncle, that Martin was not in any way committed to her, his childhood friend, but nothing could wipe away her hatred. She grieved for Martin, would always grieve, but she hated Nick Martella as she had never in her life hated. His dark power seemed to have cast a cloud over her since she had first seen him.

Tears stung her eyes, burning, bright and painful. They misted the scene she watched, the great sweep of green lawn that fell away from the old Elizabethan manor-house and reached to the lake at the edge of the park. The old stone balustrades were mellow in the sunlight, the azaleas and rhododendrons glowing, almost unreal. Yes, it was a spectacular house, and small wonder that Nick Martella had chosen it as the place where his niece would hold her wedding reception.

It was true, of course; her stepfather could refuse him nothing at all. Calvert Aircraft Components was barely hanging on in this competitive age. Martella was a giant in his sphere, a millionaire many times over, who had been invited here by her stepfather and had been coming ever since, charmed by the house. He had asked to hold business conferences here when he was in England; the size of the house made it possible and it had suited her stepfather because it had certainly brought plenty of business his way.

Until now it had meant absolutely nothing to Joanna except that she thought of Nick Martella as a dark threat. He had ignored her in his lordly way but she had never quite been able to ignore him.

When she had first seen him, at seventeen, he had frightened her. After each visit his dark, handsome face had lingered in her mind. Later she had always been glad when the conferences had been held when she was at college and she had been able to miss the whole thing, the endless number of guests, the house parties that followed. If she was at home she had made quite sure that Martin was there because she didn't like to even speak to Nick Martella and she could hardly be rude—her stepfather quite obviously needed the Martella business, hence this ready agreement to have the reception here.

Now, without a word, without a sign, he had ruined her life. It was idiotic to blame him, but she did. He was the one who had lured Martin away from the small firm of accountants where he worked. It was Martella who had inveigled Martin into joining his own firm, going to the London office to work. That was where Martin had met Rina. It all seemed deliberate, but how could it have been? It was Martin's choice and Martin had made it.

Joanna felt now that she had nobody. Martin had been her life. To the outside world she appeared to have everything: a beautiful home, a sophisticated mother whose success as a hostess was legendary, a kindly stepfather who denied her nothing. In reality, though, she had always felt lost, an outsider. Her parents had been divorced when she was eight and she had wanted to go with her father. Charles Denton was a writer, successful, famous even, but her mother had won custody.

A writer of thrillers about the world of big business was not felt to compare with the comfort that would be given to a small child at Hemmington Manor, to the steady influence that her mother and Frederick Calvert could offer. Charles Denton did a lot of roaming about, gathering material for his books in many cities of the world. He didn't even live in England permanently. He had a London flat that rarely saw him. His home was in the Caribbean, on the beautiful island of Santa Marta.

Oh, she saw him, was greatly attached to him, but he was never *there*, never close to hand when she had some problem. Eve Calvert was not the sort of mother who discussed problems, and her stepfather felt it his duty not to intrude. Basically she had always been alone except for Martin. Now she was alone completely.

Joanna blinked back her tears and walked to the mirror, sweeping her hair into a high arc, fastening the flowers securely and then allowing the cloudy golden mane to fall around one shoulder. The scent of the flowers seemed to fill the room. Lilies of the valley, costly and out of season, a sickly perfume to her nostrils. Her stomach heaved with tension and she tore them off, tossing them to the floor, securing her hair with a black velvet band. Black was more fitting than flowers, the way she felt.

The steady buzz of engines came across the park, their growing glamour filling the air, and Joanna stepped back to her window, her eyes opening in amazement to see three helicopters approaching the great front lawns, their flight like angry dragon-flies. The great man! Who else? He was here, bringing the bride, and now she would have to go down. She would have to face them, but most of all she would have to face Martin.

She saw the guests begin to descend, people she had never seen before, friends of the mighty Martella clan, elegant, wealthy people, like film stars, glittering, assured. A few of them had the dark good looks of Nick Martella, Italian-Americans, alien and worrying to her English mind. None, though, had the quiet arrogance of the man himself, none had his devastating presence.

He stepped down then, the man with dark glittering eyes, with hair like a raven's wing. Even from here she could see the handsome aesthetic face, the dark straight brows, the long firm mouth, the power that radiated around him. He held up his arms and lifted a girl out, a fairy-tale vision in white lace, her veil all-concealing, like some creature being led to her doom, except it was not doom: she was being led to Martin, to be his wife.

Joanna watched, her fist pressed to her mouth, stifling the cry that had almost escaped, as Nick Martella let his niece stand and took her arm most gently. He was wicked, powerful, an enemy, someone who had stepped out of her blackest dreams and injured her. She watched with panic-filled eyes. There was no person she could turn to, nobody to rush to, no one to take her hand.

Nick Martella smiled across and raised his hand as another man stepped down from one of the helicopters and Joanna's heart leapt with joy for one wild moment. Daddy! If there was one person left in the world she could trust, one person she had always been able to trust, then he was arriving now. How had he known? How had he got here?

She lifted her long skirts and ran from the room, biting back tears. Nothing could save her happiness, but she could hide behind her father. Somebody was on her side and it was all she needed. She was not some teenager, after all. She was twenty-three, talented, successful. All she had to do was tell herself that and cling to her father.

She flew across the lawn, her eyes steadfastly on the tall, smiling man who stood and watched her. Charles Denton was the image of the successful writer. His books were often filmed and he was well known now, not struggling as he had been when the divorce had been finalised. Now he would have won his battle to keep her. He would have thrown money into the ring as Frederick Calvert had done to please his bride-to-be. Life would have been different. She would have felt that she belonged. There would have been no Martin, no heartbreak, only the island and the sunny waters.

'Daddy!'

She threw herself into his arms and he hugged her close, chuckling in the old way, his arms a haven of comfort.

'Well, now, cherub. You didn't expect me?'

'Oh, Daddy! How could I have expected you? How was I to know that...?'

'Nick had me flown over in one of his planes.' He put his arm round her and began to walk towards the house. 'I thought he might have mentioned it. Naturally I wanted to see Rina married. I've become quite fond of her. She's a very sweet girl, a bit young perhaps, but then...'

Joanna was hardly listening. Her eyes were held by the dark eyes of the man who waited for them, watching her steadily. A shiver passed over her skin. Was her father scooped into his net too? She hadn't even known they were more than politely acquainted, yet her father was fond of the bride, had been flown out here almost as if he were enmeshed in the Martella legend and nothing to her at all.

'A whirlwind greeting.' The dark, husky voice was part of her dreaded dreams. 'I have never before seen her lose her cool dignity.' His black eyes swept over her, seeing the stifled tears, the tightly held-in emotion. They narrowed almost imperceptibly and Joanna found her hands clenching on her father's arm.

'My daughter, after all.' Charles Denton smiled, his arm still around Joanna's slender waist. 'How do you expect her to greet me? Now, if it had been Eve...'

'I cannot imagine Mrs Calvert running into any man's arms,' the husky voice noted. He turned back to Joanna, his dark eyes fastening on her face, meeting her clear gaze. 'You will look after the bride for me? She is, as you may imagine, nervous. I'm relying on you to take her in hand. It is not a man's job; at least, not until she is married and in her husband's arms.'

There was the cut of deliberate cruelty, and it seemed that every bit of colour left Joanna's face as she turned to the house, seeing the bride standing alone at the great doors. She looks lost, Joanna thought, like me.

'Perhaps she could have expected your support for a few seconds more,' she managed stiffly. 'I didn't really need to be reminded of my duties.'

Her father had been called by one of the guests and Joanna found herself alone with Nick Martella. She moved forward quickly, trying to free herself of the dark radiance, but he kept pace with her with no trouble at all, his tall, lean height almost menacing.

'You perhaps think it an imposition that I wished to hold the reception here at your home? Rina is studying in London and staying at my London home. It is not the most fitting background for a wedding. She wanted something special.'

'Brides get married from their own homes normally,' Joanna murmured through stiff lips. 'I'm surprised she didn't go back to America, but it's no imposition to me, Mr Martella. This is my stepfather's home.'

'And yours. You don't wish to attend the bride?'

'My mother asked me, and—and so did Martin, because we've always been friends. I agreed. If you don't mind, I'll get on with my duties.'

His hand came to her arm as she made to walk away.

'She is very young—nineteen. She means a great deal to me and I would not like her to be upset.'

'What makes you imagine she'll be upset, Mr Martella?' Joanna enquired coldly. 'She's getting married, the happiest day of her life. Or do you imagine that *I'll* upset her?'

'No. You're well brought up, sensitive, dignified. I don't think you would willingly upset anyone. I'm merely concerned for Rina.' His hand was firm on her arm and Joanna felt waves of revulsion shudder through her. He was powerful, self-possessed—even in her own home, the master.

'As you know my sensitivity,' she managed tightly, 'then there's nothing to fear.'

'I don't fear, Joanna. I observe and retaliate.'

The jade-green eyes slanted a look of dislike at him. He had called her Joanna. He had never done that before. It made her pull her arm away impatiently, even if he did think she was rude. His voice worried her. Deep, dark and American, with some underlying trace of accent. It should have been pleasing to the ear, but to her it was frightening.

'You're nothing to do with me, Mr Martella,' she reminded him coldly. 'My stepfather offered the hall for the wedding, and I don't particularly like being threatened, especially when I've no intention of doing anything wrong.'

'I'm no threat to you, Joanna. The threat I represent is merely in your lively imagination.'

She almost gasped. Did he know her dark dreams? How could he possibly? The night-dark eyes held hers for a second, and then she turned and swiftly walked to the house, aware of the thoughtful looks that followed her, stifling the feeling that she should run. Many people would run at a look from Nick Martella, but she wasn't going to be one of them.

Rina was in the hall, looking curiously lost, her white veil still hiding her face. Joanna felt everything tighten up inside. Was she supposed to smile, to be a happy companion for this girl? She couldn't!

'We have a room prepared for you.' She despised herself for the tight way the words came out. It wasn't this girl's fault that Martin was leaving her; not her fault either that her uncle was Nick Martella. 'It's quiet upstairs, and you can—er—get yourself together before we go across to the church.' She forced a smile and saw dark eyes watching her through the heavy lace of the veil.

The girl just followed obediently, glad to have someone to hang on to, it seemed. Clearly her uncle had deserted her, and Joanna felt another burst of anger against the arrogant man. He thought he could just issue orders and then stand back and watch. It was a wonder he hadn't ordered her stepfather to give the bride away.

The anger faded, though, as she led Rina to a small room at the back of the house, already prepared, a tranquil resting place that overlooked the woods.

'You'll be able to have a quiet minute here,' she murmured, showing the girl into the room. She was not prepared for the sight of the pale face as Rina Martella threw her veil back and regarded her with large dark eyes.

'Thank you. You're kind. You're Martin's friend?'

She looked terrified, unsure of herself, such a contrast to her overwhelming relative, and Joanna felt a twinge of conscience. She had been waiting to hate this girl, but what was there to hate?

'Yes. I'm Martin's friend. We've known each other from childhood. Sit down and have a rest. I'll get you some tea, or coffee.' Faced with the situation, she was surprised to find herself calm. The grief was there and would never go, but it was less of a dread now. She would live through it because she must, and this girl looked so helpless.

Joanna couldn't remember ever feeling helpless herself—until today. When she had been nineteen she had been completely sure of her life. Her dress designs had already been selling before she had even finished her training, and her time was spent between college and home, every minute happy because Martin was there. This girl looked as if she was accustomed to unhappiness. Her uncle's wealth had not shielded her from some misfortune and that was clear. There was actual misery in the dark eyes, not just the thought of facing the ceremony.

'Will you help me?' She was almost pathetic, and Joanna bit her lip in vexation. Why me? Her mind refused to accept the irony of it. Her beautiful mouth twisted ruefully and she managed a smile.

'Yes, of course I'll help you. There's really nothing to worry about. It's only bridal nerves.'

Her own words almost made her laugh. Bridal nerves! She was falling apart inside, dreading her own reaction as she watched Martin marry someone else, and here she was, offering solace.

Later Joanna wondered how she had managed. The wedding was beautiful, and she had stood behind the bride and carried out her duties, her mind quite blank.

As Nick Martella had brought Rina to the church door he had looked steadily at Joanna as if he expected her to start shouting, and as he handed Rina over to Martin and then sat to the side Joanna could feel his eyes on her relentlessly, but there had been a feeling of unreality that anaesthetised her to some extent. It was only as she saw Martin, his new bride on his arm, that she felt the shuddering blow of the fact that he was lost to her forever. She wanted to cry, to run away, to scream out a denial, but she was forced to stay and see it through.

And Nick Martella was there all the time, a man impossible to ignore. There was a sort of dark power about him, a splendour, alert, dark eyes that saw everything— far too much. Vitality radiated from him, and Joanna felt the jolt of it each time their eyes met. He could see her hatred, her antagonism, and she could not hide it away because now, after all the years, it was right out in the open, but he seemed to be willing her to keep upright, to control her mad urge to run, and she managed, more to defy him than anything else. She was kept on her feet by pride and a determination to get the better of him, because he *knew*, she was sure of that.

There were guests from America who had been flown in, as her grandfather had been; there were guests from London. Martin's friends had also come, and a few friends of her mother who had wanted to see this spectacle. Back at the reception, Joanna held herself aloof, living on her own kind of nervous energy, knowing that only her ability to throw herself headlong into any project would keep her sane this day.

She certainly attended the bride, and Rina's gratitude was almost tangible. It was only when it was over that Joanna felt any fear, and panic at her inability to carry on. She had seen it all happen, watched it out to the end. She was at her lowest ebb.

She stood at the side of the room, the old ballroom of this beautiful house where all the guests now danced and where Rina, now securely with Martin, looked flushed and happy.

'Well, that was really something,' one of Martin's friends sidled up to her and murmured in her ear. At least she assumed it was intended to be a murmur, but several people heard and looked round. They also heard his next remark. 'We all imagined it would be you and Martin. You've been thick as thieves since childhood. Came as a shock to find him marrying this Italian kid.'

'She's American.' Joanna stood stiffly, ready to cry, and hard arms came round her.

'Dance with me.'

The order took her by surprise, but Joanna had no time to protest. The arms held her, drew her forward, and she found herself looking up into the handsome, enigmatic face of Nick Martella as he drew her to the floor and mingled with the other guests.

It was pointless to protest. She could see that at once. Any refusal would create a scene, and she was at great pains to see this day through and then hide in her room to lick her wounds, great as they were. Many eyes were on them, the tall, dark man and the slender girl with shining golden hair, and Joanna was too shy to think of throwing any sort of fit of rage.

'I'm proud of you.' His dark eyes met her green, antagonistic gaze without flinching. 'A heart, as you will find, is never broken.'

'It's difficult to follow your chain of thought, Mr Martella,' Joanna murmured, looking quickly away.

'Not for you.' His hand turned her face back to him. 'Today you expected to die of a broken heart. You have not,' he pointed out drily. 'Instead you committed yourself to Rina and survived, as I knew you would.'

'I haven't the vaguest idea what you're talking about.' Joanna met his gaze fearlessly, but the night-black eyes burned into her own and she had to look away.

'Don't pretend with me, Joanna,' he murmured huskily. 'You imagine yourself in love with the boy. You are not. Love is entirely imagination, a vague mystical feeling that lives for a very short time indeed. You needed to get through this day, to see it happen before your eyes. I arranged that and you have survived.'

Joanna just looked at him coldly, summoning all her strength to meet the dark gaze, and his lips twisted wryly.

'You are stubborn. You don't intend to ask questions, but your eyes are alive with enquiry. I will explain. Rina had seen a photograph of this house and decided that a reception here would be spectacular. I like to indulge her, but I could have refused. I could have taken over any hotel in London for this wedding. Alternatively I could have flown every guest to America. I chose to have the ceremony and the reception here instead because you needed to face the fact that Martin Sutton is married to Rina and no longer available for any dreams. You needed to see him married and now you have. I'm proud of you, as I said. Now you may forget him. You don't love him. It was a child's dream, a dream you should have grown out of a long time ago.'

Joanna was too shocked to make any pronouncement at all. He had done all the pronouncing and her mind could hardly take it all in. He was telling her very categorically that he had engineered all this, all this torture, for her sake alone.

'How dare you speak to me like that?' She tried to pull away, but his strength was too great, a conquering strength that held her fast, his hands tightly at her waist, his eyes burning into her.

'I will speak to you as I choose!' His lips tightened at her anger. 'The bride is there for you to see. It is finished, over. Forget him. I would not have allowed it in any case, even if Rina had not existed. You're *mine*, exactly what I want.'

Her knees seemed to be ready to buckle under her. The dark eyes held hers effortlessly, the hands that clasped her turned her back into his arms as she tried to pull away.

'Let me go!' She said the words through clenched teeth, afraid she would scream out her denial if she let herself go, but he merely smiled, that cold dark smile she had seen many times before.

'If I let you go it will merely be on a temporary basis.'

He looked down at her steadily and she seemed to be hypnotised, a rabbit with a fox, and suddenly the smile softened, the white teeth showed against the tanned skin of his face, the hard lips quirked.

'I frighten you, Joanna? You tremble like a leaf in the breeze. I'm not threatening to kidnap you. It will not take too long before you're willing. I will make you want me as you never dreamed to want a man before.'

'Y-you're disgusting!' The words came out more shakily than she would have liked, but he relaxed his hold, the long lips quirking again.

'Merely determined,' he corrected. 'I have imagination too. I have imagined you beside me in the night, your golden hair on my pillow, your slender body locked in my arms. I am not a man to live on imagination indefinitely. I prefer reality. I will give you a few weeks to grow accustomed to the idea.'

'You may be mad, Mr Martella,' Joanna said in a taut voice, 'but I'm not mad at all. It may have escaped your notice for six years, but I don't like you in the least. In fact, this little experiment of today has more than confirmed that.'

'It was not an experiment. It was a thing you had to face, to rid you of this ridiculous notion of love for a childhood friend. And call me Nick. Polite English formality can become tiresome.'

'Not as tiresome as your insane humour, Mr Martella!' Joanna snapped.

'If you believe it's humour, then why are you afraid?' he asked softly. 'Why do you tremble?' His hand tightened on her wrist as she tore herself away. 'I'm not joking, Joanna. I want you, and anything I want, I get, I never let go. It's part of my nature.'

Joanna pulled away and he let her go, but his eyes followed her with brilliant determination and she dared not simply leave the room. Too many people were watching, intrigued by the small scene they could only conjecture about. Her mother's eyes were intent on her pale face, and Martin was looking at her with an enquiry that told its own story. She fled to her father and danced with him, her body slowly coming back to life, her trembling subsiding.

'You've been overdoing it,' Charles Denton said quietly. 'I've watched you throw yourself into this day like a lunatic. What's come over you?'

'Well, I never let the side down, Daddy. You know that.'

'Never let Eve down, you mean,' he grunted. 'I don't know why she wanted this wedding here. She doesn't know a soul except the few cronies of hers, and she's deeply affronted that I'm here. Nick could have held this in London, at the Savoy, I expect.'

'So he said,' Joanna murmured, keeping her eyes lowered when she found that black, brilliant gaze still on her.

'Well, Eve usually gets her way,' Charles muttered, but Joanna almost laughed hysterically. Not with Nick Martella! He demanded something and he got it, especially with her stepfather, who was going around looking very honoured. Nick Martella had arranged all this for one purpose. She would have been inclined to think him demented, but his dark eyes told her he was not. Her nightmares were out in the open now. No doubt Freddy would gain some business advantage and think himself duly blessed. Nobody knew what it was all about, nobody but Nick Martella and her.

CHAPTER TWO

EVE CALVERT came up and leaned over to peck at Joanna's cheek as the music stopped for a moment.

'Well done, darling. You looked wonderful, much more beautiful than the bride. I did think that Martin dithered a bit in church, didn't you?'

Joanna was once again speechless. Everything just slid by her mother unless she particularly wanted to see it. Any normal mother would have known how her daughter felt. And it looked as if she wasn't about to even acknowledge her ex-husband. She did, though. Apparently he was not a social success.

'This is a bit over the top, Charles, isn't it?' She frowned at him, clearly indicating that he should not be here, and he took the attitude he always took, one of deliberate misunderstanding.

'Oddly enough, I agree with you,' he murmured, looking round the room. 'I can never understand anyone hanging on to these hideous, historical old heaps. Still, I suppose it's been in Fred's family for generations?'

It was the nearest Joanna had come to laughing in weeks. Her stepfather was Frederick, of enormous importance, according to her mother. In private, Joanna thought of him as Freddy and from time to time she called him that, never in her mother's presence. Now he was plain Fred, and Eve's face tried its best to redden with annoyance but refused to allow such indignity.

'Impossible man!' she hissed. 'I never cease to understand why I divorced you.' She swept away, across the room, and Joanna rested her head against her father's

23

shoulder, wishing with all her heart that he had won custody of her so long ago.

'Oh, Daddy! You're a wicked man. I'll never hear the last of that.'

He tipped her smiling face up and grinned down at her. 'Terrible woman, your mother. Can't stand her. How about flying back with me to Santa Marta? Nick will fly you back with me with no trouble. Did he tell you he's bought that old Spanish fort above the bay? He had a battle to get permission but he won, of course. He's restored it beautifully. It's a fantastic house now. Only a man with his amount of wealth could have done it.'

It brought Joanna back to life.

'He lives on Santa Marta? I thought he lived in New York.'

'Not permanently. Not for a couple of years. Of course, he's always in and out. He never has a lot of time, but what time he has he spends on the island. I suppose he's now the best friend I have. He plays a devilish game of chess.'

He would, being the devil! Joanna felt her heart sink, desolation racing back. Nick Martella had taken everything from her, almost isolated her. His niece had married Martin. He had bought a piece of the most beautiful island in the world where she had spent so many happy hours, and now he had taken her father. Hatred came flooding back, hatred that had been submerged for a while in shock and fear. He was surrounding her! She had the terrible feeling that she would have to fight him right out in the open at some point, and she shuddered at the thought.

When the bridal pair was ready to leave she had one last duty. She went back to the room that Rina had used and helped her to get ready.

'You've been a good friend to me today, Joanna.' The dark eyes looked at Joanna and smiled. 'I was so scared. Now I'm happy and I feel I've made a friend. You're now not just Martin's friend. We'll have lots of outings together after our honeymoon, and you must bring your boyfriend.'

'Oh, I will,' Joanna murmured, her eyes hidden, her lips threatening to tremble. She hurried Rina into her clothes and almost thrust her out on to the passage. 'Go down. I'll—I'll come in a minute.'

She turned to the bed where the bridal gown lay, so white and delicate, her hands reluctant to lift it and hang it up. It should have been her! It should be Joanna and Martin going away, not this girl with soft eyes. A sob rose in her throat and she spun round defensively as she heard a slight noise at the open door.

'Jo! I can't really believe I'm going off without you.' Martin stood there and smiled ruefully at her. 'Somehow it's like a fairy-tale, not quite true.'

It was like a nightmare to her, but Joanna tried to smile. She wanted to run into his arms, put her fingers to the thick fair hair. He just didn't know what this was doing to her.

'You've just missed the bride,' she managed gaily. 'I sent her down a minute ago.'

'I know. I saw her go. I was wanting to say goodbye to you, to thank you for...' He suddenly closed his eyes and grimaced, looking across at her then with something like despair on his face. 'You just watched it all, Jo. I was looking at you and you never flinched.'

'What did you expect me to do, attack the bride?' Joanna stood like a statue, stiff and tight, holding herself together, not even letting her face relax, and he shrugged, back to looking rueful.

'I don't know what I expected—something, after all
the time you and I——'

'Your wife is waiting for you,' an icy voice said, and
over Martin's shoulder Joanna saw Nick Martella appear,
silently and threateningly. She also saw Martin pale
visibly.

'I know. Just saying thank you to Joanna.' He looked
across at her, wanting to say more but clearly not daring.
Now he was one of Martella's men, a minion, taking
orders. He just turned and left, and Joanna faced Nick
Martella as he stood at the door, making no attempt to
go downstairs with Martin.

'How fortunate that he merely stayed at the door.' He
didn't have to enlarge on that, the softly sinister un-
dertone was quite enough, and Joanna stared at him,
almost hypnotised. He suddenly relaxed, a very clear decision on his part. 'It's over, Joanna. Forget him. You're
pale, distressed, but it will pass and you will look back
and see how foolish all this was, how much wasted
emotion.'

'I don't have emotions,' Joanna managed, choking
back the tears. 'I would be grateful, Mr Martella, if you
would go downstairs and leave me to put these things
away.'

'Nick,' he corrected quietly. 'As to your emotions, they
show in your face, in those amazing eyes. One day soon
those eyes will change colour and glow for me.'

'They already have done,' Joanna snapped, rage sur-
facing. 'I never liked you, Mr Martella, and now I can
only think I hate you. If I should ever know that you're
coming here again I'll make quite sure I'm a long way
off!'

He took one menacing step towards her and Joanna
backed away, her expression of loathing making his face
harden frighteningly.

'I will not touch you,' he grated angrily. 'I will merely tell you this: I leave for America tomorrow. I shall be there for two months. When I return I intend to come for you.'

The thought of people in the house left Joanna's head entirely. Her hands clenched at her sides and her considerable temper surfaced over grief, fear and utter bewilderment.

'If you were the last man in the universe I wouldn't consent to be near you!' she shouted. 'You've taken away everything I've ever wanted. You've even sneaked up and taken my father. Now I can never go to Santa Marta again!'

'I know you love the island,' he said with surprising quiet. 'Your father told me. We will live there and you will see your father whenever you care to walk down the beach to his house.'

'I'll see him when he comes over to England,' Joanna corrected bitterly. 'One thing is for sure, though: after today I'll never see *you* again! Forget the mad idea about me, Mr Martella, because I'd rather die!'

'You will not die, Joanna,' he said silkily, 'unless it is the small death that lovers die in each other's arms. And I intend to be your lover. In two months I will be back.'

He turned and walked out, and Joanna sank to the bed, careless of the fact that she was crushing the beautiful gown, her legs shaking too much to hold her up any more. When she finally drummed up enough courage to go back down, the wedding party was ready to leave, and she stood dutifully close to her mother as they all made their farewells, the only time for many years she had felt in need of her mother's protection.

He came, of course, to thank her mother and stepfather, to take her hand and offer his congratulations

of a job well done, but his eyes were cold and dark, no
trace of the burning fire in them that had outraged and
frightened her. Rina came and thanked her again, but
Martin stayed away, his eyes on Joanna's pale face, and
she knew he dared not even shake her hand. Nick
Martella was watching, his eyes like chips of ice, black
and bottomless.

The helicopters lifted off in perfect unison and her
shoulders fell with relief, anger and grief flooding over
her when she realised that for the last two hours she had
thought very little of Martin and her lost love. She re-
sented the fact that it was Nick Martella who had got
her through this day. Her hatred for him had kept her
tears at bay.

When she went to her room finally she found a card
slipped under the door. It was written in a firm and un-
compromising hand.

Come to me, or I will come for you.

Dramatic swine! He had even invaded her privacy. She
could almost feel him here in her room, although he had
merely pushed the card beneath her door. No doubt he
had discovered where she slept from his many visits here.
It made her feel unsafe and more angry than ever, more
surrounded. His London address and telephone number
were on the card, and she started to tear it up, but some
impulse stopped her. Maybe she would sneak up there
one night and poison him. She pushed it into a drawer
and tried to forget all about it. She had enough grief to
contemplate and, now that she was alone, the tears came,
fast and hot. It felt like the end of her life.

Next day Joanna walked into the shop looking tired and
pale. Eileen Gordon looked up and then went on staring
at her. She knew Joanna well. They had been at design

school together, although Eileen had been one year ahead
of Joanna. By the time Joanna was finished Eileen had
set up this boutique with very little money, and Joanna
had come in with her as a partner. They sold their own
designs and creations. It had been a risky venture but it
had worked so far, and now Joanna's designs were selling
much further afield. It would have been quite easy to
let the whole thing take off, to become quite wealthy on
the Joanna Denton label, but Joanna preferred it here.
Buyers came down from London frequently, but here
was the hub of the whole thing, a safe place as far as
Joanna was concerned.

'You look awful,' Eileen muttered, watching with
friendly disquiet.

'I had a pretty bad night.' Her pale face told its own
story and Eileen looked slightly embarrassed.

'Too much champagne, I expect. Did it go all right?'

'Naturally. When my mother organises something it
stays organised.' Joanna sounded a little bitter, and
Eileen glanced at her anxiously.

'Come into the back and have a cup of tea. We don't
need to open yet.'

'It's nearly nine.'

'Then we'll open at ten past. If anyone knocks I'll
come back in.'

Joanna didn't feel up to facing customers anyhow, so
she went through to the back room where they had lunch,
designed clothes and generally conducted their affairs.

'He wasn't really your type, Jo,' Eileen pointed out
quietly after a minute. 'It would have been a big mistake.'

'May I know what you're talking about?' Joanna
looked carefully into her cup. Did everyone know about
her love for Martin? Was her guilty secret no secret at
all?

'I'm talking about Martin Sutton and you damned well know it!' Eileen glared at her frustratedly. 'I've known you a long time, Joanna, and I've never ceased to hear about Martin, the dream-boy. He wasn't your type.'

'Really, Eileen! I don't know what——'

'Put a sock in it,' Eileen bit out rudely. She pushed her round glasses up on her nose. 'You were going to marry Martin when you were a teenager; only trouble was, he didn't know it. Anybody who turns you down has to be a drip; therefore, he's one!'

'We were just—just friends,' Joanna began, choking back tears.

'Obviously. Your friend got married and you waved him off. I can see you're very satisfied about it.'

Tears spilled over on to Joanna's cheeks and she turned away frantically. It wasn't only that. Losing Martin had devastated her, but she had not even been able to mourn in peace. It was this feeling of being menaced, pursued, threatened.

'Oh, Joanna! I'm a bitch.' Eileen put her arm around Joanna and clucked at her like a small, plump hen, and it helped. Joanna dried her eyes and sniffed ruefully.

'No. You're quite right. It's better to face facts. I'm an idiot.'

'Now I never said that,' Eileen pointed out righteously. 'Martin Sutton's the idiot, and he's all wrong for you anyway. You need someone very special.'

'Martin's special; there's nobody else who can even begin to match up to him,' Joanna managed with a tearful smile, and Eileen gave a very theatrical sniff.

'He's a drip; he's now married. How can you go on saying he's special when he let you down? Look around for Prince Charming.'

'No, thanks,' Joanna stated grimly. 'From this day forth and until further notice I'm a business lady.'

'Amen,' Eileen murmured. 'Get cracking—that's the door.'

It was the start of a surprisingly busy day, and Joanna tried hard to lose herself in it. She never quite managed. A dark, handsome face kept coming into her mind. The wedding seemed to still hang in the air, but more than that her own private space had been infiltrated.

She felt she had to keep away from the manor. She was breathlessly aware that Nick Martella had been in the house and, looking back, she realised she had always felt like that. Even when she had been away and a conference had been held at home, she had sensed his presence long after, had never needed to be informed that he had been there. His personality seemed to hang around after he had gone. She had often wondered if this was how he stole into her disturbed dreams, dreams she had had off and on since she had first seen him.

She had dreamed again last night and this was really the cause of her misery today, the true basis for her tears, if she would admit it. The dream had been different. This time the pursuing figure had caught her, crushed her against him, kissed her cruelly, and she had *liked* it! She had shot up in bed in her darkened room at five this morning and had not slept since, the dream lingering in her mind, troubling her body because she could still feel those hard arms, that insistent mouth.

She had stumbled into the shower and turned on the water, standing in her nightie as the cooling spray had dashed over her, trembling to discover that her breasts were swollen and tight, her tummy muscles tensed with a peculiar pain. There had been a melting sensation right through her, new and frightening, as if she had no control over her own body.

She had never felt like that before and the feeling had taken a long time to fade. She was safer here in the shop, surrounded by interested customers. Eileen was extremely down to earth. She probably didn't dream at all, and if she did it would be a dream of swirling colour, brilliant jackets and long, swinging skirts.

She was a designer too, already quite well known. Why did she have to dream of a dark, lean face, of black, glittering eyes, a cruel mouth that came closer with every dream? She shuddered. It was the result of hatred. She would have to look it up.

'Do you ever dream, Eileen?' she asked quietly during a lull in trade when Eileen was busily lifting clothes back to the racks, looking for faults as usual.

'Hmm! Big fashion shows, world acclaim, TV interviews.'

Joanna smiled and breathed a sigh of relief. Sanity had spoken, even if it was a very unusual kind of sanity. The hell with Nick Martella!

She regretted that thought a few weeks later. Just as she was leaving the shop Eileen stopped her.

'Can you hang on a minute, Joanna? I've got something to tell you and I've been mulling it around in my head all day. I don't know quite what to do and I certainly don't want to let you down.'

Joanna turned back into the shop and somehow she knew she had a problem, another one. Why was it that a dark, handsome face appeared in her mind whenever things looked worrying? He couldn't reach out here to her. In any case, he'd probably have forgotten all about her now. She hadn't forgotten about him. The dreams were still there, real and painful; Martin seemed to be no longer one of them. Even when she was awake, his face was blurred in her mind, overshadowed by another face, a strong, determined face.

'If I can help?' Joanna sat on the edge of the counter and looked at her friend, seeing anxiety and embarrassment flit across the usually calm expression.

'I may as well get it right out,' Eileen said ruefully. 'Fact is, Joanna, I've been offered a great deal of money for the premises. Why anyone would want such a tiny place is beyond me, but the price is—well—astonishing.'

'What about the business?' Joanna realised she was almost holding her breath. Take this away and she was out into the wide, wide world. She would have to go round and sell her designs, make up a portfolio, be a businesswoman. She was too shy. She did not in any way own the premises. The money she had put in had been all for equipment and materials and, although they both knew that it was Joanna's designs that made the wheels go round, Joanna had never wanted to take matters further. People had to come to her. She just could not push herself, sell herself.

'You know my dad lent me the money for this the year before you came in,' Eileen reminded her. 'He had to borrow himself to do it, but that's Dad. I've been paying it back bit by bit but it eats into the profits, and there's no chance to expand although we're bursting at the seams here. Well, if I sell out to this firm we've been offered rented property in London, in a fabulous spot, a sure winner. I could pay Dad back, have some capital and set up in a good area. With the name you're making for yourself it would go a bomb.'

'Who's offering the property?' Joanna asked with a feeling of fright. She just couldn't help this suspicion. She was dogged by a demon. In her heart she knew it.

'The same company that wants to buy this. It doesn't make a lot of sense to me, but I expect they know their own business. The trouble is, would you go to London with me? It would mean getting living accommodation and being all at sixes and sevens for a while.'

'What's the name of the company?' Joanna persisted. She expected to hear Martella Industries, was sure of it for some reason, but it was not that at all.

'Er—Micro-Consolidates,' Eileen read from her notepad by the phone. 'Funny name, but interesting money. Look,' she added as Joanna sat there, unable to believe it, the chills down her spine beginning to fade, 'it's Friday tomorrow. Let's both think about it over the weekend. We'll have a conference on Monday. We'll decide whether we're going to go big or stay here.'

All the way home Joanna chased it around in her head. It was all very straightforward. Some firm wanted to start up here in this little town. It sounded like a computer firm. Well, there was not one computer shop here and that annoyed some people. It ought to do well. In London too her name could only grow. So why were her instincts still at full alert? Why was that face swimming round in her mind?

When she got her stepfather to herself for a minute after dinner she asked him for the information.

'Freddy, have you ever heard of Micro-Consolidates?'

'Maybe. Just a minute.' He was always interested in business and left the room to go to his study, coming back after a minute with a thick book. 'Here we are; thought as much. It's part of Martella Industries. That man has a hand in everything. I mean—"industries" covers a big field as a name. Interesting fella. Started from nothing, back streets of New York, grandparents Italian from the old country. I understand he was a millionaire times over by the time he was twenty-five. Well, I mean, he *must* have been. He was coming to this house when he was about twenty-eight. You were seventeen then, probably didn't notice him. Lord knows what he's worth now.'

Joanna wasn't really listening. She didn't want to know. And she certainly had noticed him when she was seventeen. She had been too young to really know what his eyes were doing to her, but she had felt threatened.

'Invited him here for the weekend as a matter of fact, but he couldn't come. Tied up, I expect.'

He ought to be! He should be tied up and dropped into some river, preferably from one of his own planes! He must be back in England. She didn't know what to say because her stepfather was in full flow, and she had to get out, to think.

'Well, thanks for the information. Eileen wanted to know, actually. They're thinking of setting a place up in town.'

She stood up and began to edge out of the room, and her stepfather reached for his drink, quite content to sit by the fire and doze.

'Good idea. Should do well. Computers and things.'

How Freddy ran a business she had never been able to fathom. He seemed utterly dreamy to Joanna. Still, they lived in the lap of luxury. Who was she to query it? She almost raced to her room, seething and thinking furiously. Wanting to get her thoughts out and place them in a neat row to examine.

They needed little examination. The two months were up and he was isolating her further. He was mad! No, it was impossible! Joanna stared at herself in the mirror and knew it was no such thing.

'Just because I'm paranoid it doesn't mean he's not after me,' she murmured. She didn't know whether to be frightened or enraged, but finally rage asserted itself and she decided to act. Hiding was over, it was over for good. In the morning she would go after *him* and see how he liked it. Two could be a nuisance. She was no longer going to sit down under this threat. In any case, seeing him again would wipe out these impossible dreams. They were beginning to take over her life, make her skin hot. It was almost indecent, as if she were sleeping with him each night.

In the morning she came down, ready to go straight from the shop. She was wearing one of her own creations, a simple grey dress with a pleated skirt that swung as she walked, showing insets of brilliantly red flowers. Her mother inspected her minutely, from her shining golden head to her dainty high heels.

'Very nice. Simple but nice,' she murmured. 'Going to town?'

'I have to go to London after work,' Joanna muttered, horrified when her face flushed. Anyone would think this was an assignation with Nick Martella, not a meeting for battle. 'I'll stay with Margaret if it gets late.'

'Oh, very well, dear.' Her mother's interest died with its usual speed. She wasn't interested in Joanna's friends, and her stepfather didn't even know they existed. Joanna had been a free agent since she was about seventeen, her work and father her only real ties, except for Martin.

Funny how it didn't hurt so much now. Eileen had driven her like a tyrant, and there had been letters and calls from people making appointments to see their latest work. She had been too tired at night to think of anything but going to sleep. The dreams had disturbed her constantly too, making her pale and listless, leaving her with a daily feeling that she had a guilty secret and a man in her life.

The evil genius had raised his head again now. He had walked right out of her dreams and this time he had gone too far. He was going to find out how much she hated him. He could just get back to New York and his beautiful women and leave her alone. She was about to put a stop to Nick Martella's attitude of take anything you want.

On the way up to London later that day Joanna's temper cooled a little. In fact she had almost decided not to come because as she had gone to her drawer and collected the card he had left she had had the awful feeling of fate taking a hand. If she had torn this card up as she had started to do she would have had no idea where to find him. Was she simply walking into his life like an idiot? The memory of his words kept her going, however. He played dark and dangerous games. He had said he wanted her and he was cutting her out like a quarry. It did not please her to feel that she was being rounded up like some defenceless creature. She was *not* defenceless!

Joanna hadn't the faintest idea really what she would say to that arrogant American. He wasn't even that, she told herself. He was a mixture, a New York Italian or some such thing. He had more arrogance than an Eastern prince and more money than was decent. All the same, she began to feel uneasy. She had set off on a wave of temper but now she had to decide on a plan of action.

Trying to reason with him would not really be wise; he was very unreasonable, after all. The best thing would be to shame him, to make him see that his attitude had finally gone over the invisible barrier of taste. He was supposed to be a friend of her father's, so he must know he couldn't do this to her. Her father would be furious if he knew. Dared she tell him, though? Her father would think it was some young girl's fantasy. Nick Martella would make quite sure he thought that.

By the time she found herself outside his door, the taxi driving off, Joanna felt as if her nerves were stretched wires. It was a very wealthy district, the house in a

curving Georgian terrace, white stone and a gracious
height, the gleaming black of the paintwork, the per-
fection of the wrought-iron railings all speaking of a
much older, more elegant age. This part of London was
still extremely elegant, though, housing several famous
people, as she knew, and her heart was beating just too
fast as she mounted the shallow steps to the door and
rang the bell.

Maybe he wasn't even here. The thought struck her
suddenly and she had no real idea as to why she should
imagine he would be back in London right on the dot,
after the two months were up. It was surely imagination,
giving herself so much importance in his life? She was
rather ashamed of the feeling of relief the thought gave
her. She was in danger of backing out of this, and she
rang the bell again before she gave up and sneaked off,
beaten. This was no attitude to take. Was she admitting
he frightened her? Yes. Her mind acknowledged it swiftly
with no thought of cowardice. He did.

What she had expected to confront her she did not
know, but the sight of a rather ugly face, greying black
hair and a grizzled chin quite took her aback. She just
stared.

'Can I help you, ma'am?'

The owner of the face peered at her rather owlishly,
and Joanna wondered who on earth he was. Surely Nick
Martella surrounded himself with the very best servants,
even a butler? If this was a butler he was a very odd-
looking one, and he was in his shirt-sleeves. They didn't
have anything so splendid as a butler at home, but if
they had had her mother would have chosen a little better
than this. He looked as if he had wandered in from the
nearest bar. Her mother would faint at the sight of him.

'I want to see Mr Martella.' She looked into his piggy little eyes with a great deal of determination, willing him to surrender, but his ugly face was unimpressed.

'Don't think you can.' He took a firm stance himself, and Joanna's green eyes narrowed ominously. Having summoned up her courage, she was going to see this thing through. And where had he got that accent? Definitely American, but a bit too nasal. He sounded like a cartoon character. She nearly smiled but held on to her wavering thoughts tightly.

'It's a matter of life and death,' she said clearly, enunciating each word carefully.

'It might be for one of us. He ain't nice when he's interrupted.'

The face in front of her remained perfectly blank, the small eyes watchful, but Joanna was filled with glee. So he *was* here? And doing something that must not be interrupted!

She had a vision of a beautiful woman. She had seen pictures of those beauties who drifted through his life, and her lips tightened determinedly. To catch him at a disadvantage would be very sweet indeed and nothing was going to stop her now. She would also tell him that she had no intention of being *his*! She would tell him right in front of the face of his startled lady-love. It seemed a blissful revenge.

'I'm a very dear friend,' she said resolutely, fixing him with an unwavering stare. 'I must see Mr Martella before—before I go back to Santa Marta. If I don't see him he'll be furious.'

He was impressed now. She could see that he was quite accustomed to fury from his boss.

'OK, but don't say I didn't warn yer.'

He opened the door wider and she stepped inside, not too sure of victory now that it was in her grasp but temper right there at the top of her feelings, burning her.

The hall was wider than she had expected, a curved wrought-iron staircase leading to the next floor, and instead of asking her to wait in some room downstairs the man signalled her forward.

'He's up here.'

He *was* in the bedroom. How delightful! She clenched her hands and prepared to face a very embarrassing scene, except that he would be the one to be embarrassed. She could already hear voices and she fought against all her good breeding. He would only be getting what he deserved. If this was unforgivable then what was he? She went up before she could change her mind. The man knocked, opened the door very wide and Joanna found herself facing several interested pairs of eyes.

It was a study. There wasn't one woman present. She had simply walked into a meeting, and she felt her face flood with colour as she realised her own temerity. What had come over her? She didn't know this man at all and yet she had more or less forced her way into his house, right into a private meeting. What was she going to say now?

CHAPTER THREE

NICK MARTELLA was sitting behind a huge mahogany desk, and when he stood up he seemed to fill the room. That inexplicable radiance seemed to reach out and touch her, and Joanna stood like stone, unable to say one word at all.

He wasn't furious, she could see that. There was a flash of something in those midnight-black eyes that was unfathomable, but his face was perfectly composed, almost aloof.

'My dear Joanna. You surprise me.'

Danger seemed to flood around her at the sound of the dark, husky voice, and she noticed the others get to their feet. Instead of interrupting a love scene she was in a room filled with polite businessmen. An enormous feeling of being trapped washed over her, of being idiotic, childish and downright impudent.

Her only thought was to escape, bury her head and hope it was a nightmare that nobody else had noticed. She turned and ran, brushing past the man at the door and making her way headlong down the stairs.

'*Joanna*!'

The sharp command merely added to her panic as she raced down the stairs, her feet hardly touching the steps. It was ridiculous. She had made a complete fool of herself because now she could not think of one single thing to say to him even if she dared to stop. Why, oh, why had she thought herself capable of bearding this particular lion in his den?

Almost at the bottom of the stairs, she slipped, her clutching hand missing the rail entirely, and the world seemed to become a topsy-turvy place as she fell down the last of the flight, her shoulders hitting the hard steps one at a time, knocking the breath from her, the pain in her back excruciating.

She opened dazed eyes and Nick Martella was there, kneeling beside her, raising her head carefully and looking annoyed beyond words.

'*Little fool*!' He stared down at her. 'Why did you run? What sort of monster do you think I am?'

'The worst.' She murmured the words as her face twisted in pain, and his frown was as black as his eyes. It was traumatic to have him so close, bending over her, touching her. It brought back all her dreams and, even through the pain, her skin tingled, heated. When she tore her gaze from his she could see interested faces peering from the height of the stairs, and Nick too seemed suddenly to become aware of them.

'Gentlemen. We will call the meeting closed.'

It was so arrogantly smooth, as if the sight of a girl at the bottom of his stairs was an everyday occurrence. He rapped out a few words to the servant, who nodded and moved away quickly. Then she had every chance to see the interested spectators, because Nick picked her up carefully and mounted the stairs towards them.

'A friend, gentlemen,' he remarked coolly. 'Obviously something has alarmed her. Obviously too she needs attention. We'll continue the discussion at Monday's meeting.'

He didn't wait for approval, not that he would, the master of the world! He shouldered a door open further along the passage and Joanna found herself being placed with a great deal of care on a soft bed. There was nothing for it but to get out the reason for her visit.

'How dare you offer to...?' Her righteous wrath deserted her as she fainted, and her last sight of him was not encouraging. She had infuriated him, even though he had kept control of that considerable temper. His lips were set in one straight line, the dark eyes narrowed and cold.

When she came round she was under the sheets. Her shoes had been removed, and she opened her eyes to find him standing at the foot of the bed, his eyes intently on her, his arms folded across his chest in an ominous manner.

'What you say now is, "Where am I?"' he suggested grimly.

'I know where I am. I didn't hit my head,' Joanna assured him shakily.

'A minor miracle. Is your behaviour normally so odd? Do you regularly insinuate yourself into the homes of people you know and then flee in terror?'

'I didn't. I saw you had a meeting and——'

'Stop being ridiculous!' he snapped impatiently. 'As you regard me as some sort of predator, you must have had a very pressing reason for coming here. You will tell me what it is.'

'Who undressed me?' Joanna suddenly realised that she was in her lacy slip and remembered too that she had seen no one here but the servant, apart from the visitors, who would hardly like to take a hand in making her comfortable.

Her anxious question brought a twisted smile to those arrogant lips and he let the question hang in the air until her pallor changed to rose-pink confusion.

'Colby has a wife,' he informed her when she seemed to be burning up with embarrassment. 'She travels with us. She prepared you for the doctor.'

'I don't need a doctor. If you'll just go out I'll——'

'The doctor is on his way. I have no intention of going out. Your peculiar ways lead me to believe that you may jump from the window. I wouldn't like it on my conscience.'

'I'm big on self-preservation,' Joanna managed, her shoulders hurting madly as she tried to move.

'I have reason to doubt it. Don't move. I don't know the extent of your injuries. It was a risk to lift you. Lie perfectly still—and be good.' He added that last with a faint smile, and Joanna glared at him.

'Will you stop talking to me as if I'm a demented child?' she snapped.

'Will you stop behaving like one?' He turned, moving to the door. 'You will have to acquire more poise. I imagined you already had poise. It will be necessary when you live with me.'

'Come back!' Joanna stormed. 'I've got several things to say to you.'

'The doctor has arrived. When he has gone I'll certainly come back.' He paused at the door, the dark eyes flashing over her. 'When I carried you upstairs I considered putting you into my own bed. The thought still hangs around in its tantalising manner.'

'You're mad!'

Her minor insult gained no reply at all. He merely slanted her a dark, amused look and left. As he closed the door on her Joanna fought back a wave of unaccustomed feeling, though not entirely unaccustomed. Her dreams seemed to be turning into reality. Her mouth felt dry, her hands trembled. She tried to get out of bed but sank back on to the soft pillows. It felt as if her shoulders had been stepped on by a horse. Far from winning any battle, she seemed to have precipitated herself into danger. There had been a chauvinistic masculine amusement at the back of those dark, intent eyes all the time.

'Multiple bruising,' the doctor pronounced after a lengthy examination. 'Nothing broken, but you'll be quite stiff for a couple of days. You're very lucky, young lady. Those stairs are hard.'

She was being chaperoned by a very firm woman, who regarded her solemnly, and as the doctor left she advanced on the bed and wrapped Joanna up.

'I'll make some tea for you, love. Then I'll get you a nightdress.'

'I can't stay here!' Joanna looked at her in horror and received a warm smile.

'You can't move yet. The doctor said so. It's going to be no trouble to look after you. Mr Martella is a very busy man, but I'm here all the time.'

Joanna just looked at her, confused thoughts wheeling through her mind, and clearly the woman thought she was still dazed. 'Love'? That's what the woman had said.

'You're English?' It suddenly dawned on her.

'Yes, I married Ed when they were over here years ago. I go all over with them. It's a great life.'

'Ed?' Joanna looked more dazed than ever.

'Colby. He let you in. He's been Mr Martella's servant for years.'

Nick came back into the room after a brief tap on the door, and the woman left with a quick smile at him. There was a subservient air about her that everyone seemed to have when he was there. Now that she looked back on it, her own mother was hard pressed not to drop him the odd curtsy. And that ugly-faced man at the door was married to that nice, calm woman? People did odd things.

Joanna went straight into the attack.

'How dare you offer to buy the shop from right under my feet?'

'Ah! You've managed to get it out at last. Am I to understand that this is the reason for your visit?'

'What else? You've cut me off from everyone I care about, and now you're taking my place of work. We don't behave like that in this country.'

'What a naïve and idiotic remark. There are businessmen in this country who make my hair stand on end. The purchase is merely a business matter. I imagined you owned half of the shop. Surely you haven't been dismissed?'

Joanna looked at him with intense dislike, and he looked back derisively.

'Eileen Gordon owns the premises, but it makes no difference. She's my friend. There's no question of dismissal, so you can forget that. Therefore, the plan, whatever it was, failed.'

'So, you're moving to London with her?'

The way he said it was quite frightening, as if he was penning her closer, and she was finding it difficult to move her gaze from his.

'I'm not moving to London. Eileen won't sell.'

'Then I must raise the price. I can afford it.'

'You're wasting your time. She won't sell and, even if she did, I wouldn't move to London. My designs are well known already. I'll just go somewhere else. You can't buy every shop in town.'

'I probably can,' he murmured sardonically. 'I had no idea you could be so amusing. There's a great deal boiling below the surface with you, Joanna. Getting to really know you is an exciting prospect. I can give you anything you want. Stop thinking of me as a threat.'

'I think of you as a monster. We've already established that. Get me my clothes!' Joanna choked out. 'I have no wish to be here.'

'Very well. I'll order the car and see you're safely delivered home.'

He walked out and the way he had simply given in left Joanna momentarily stunned. She had expected an argument, a direct refusal. She had expected some reference to his threat, but here he was, just letting her go. It was idiotically disappointing, as if a spark of fire had died. What was wrong with her? She must be going mad too.

She climbed gingerly out of bed and as her feet touched the floor they gave way beneath her and she sank to the carpet with a low moan of pain.

'Oh!' She bit her lip, pain forcing tears into her eyes, and when she opened them he was standing in the doorway, a look of extreme irritation on his face.

'You are stupid! Small wonder you imagined yourself in love with that simpering boy!' He strode across to her angrily and she looked up at him with pain-filled eyes, the vivid jade-green awash with tears.

'He's not too simpering to be taken on as part of your firm, is he? Not too simpering to marry your niece. You did it on purpose, didn't you? You deliberately took him away and introduced him to another lifestyle, to your niece, and all the glamour that surrounds you!'

'Yes. I did.' His face looked down at her, his expression utterly cold. 'I want you myself and I have very good reasons for my choice. I generally remove obstacles that stand in my way. What has he lost? He's married to an heiress, his life henceforth extremely comfortable.'

'What about me? What about my loss?' Joanna asked bitterly, and he glared down at her.

'Explain your loss to me after a month in my care, after nights in my arms. The matter is ended, and so is your foolish escape. You have some growing up to do. You will stay here and then go with me to Santa Marta.'

'You've kidnapped me?' Joanna looked at him with great distaste, but he simply bent and lifted her effortlessly, placing her back on the bed.

'If the idea excites you then—yes.' His eyes slid over her, slowly making her aware of her state of dress. 'Didn't I tell you you would come to me? Here you are. In a moment Nora will bring you two pain-killers the doctor left for you. Tomorrow we'll talk, when you're less filled with pain and annoyance.'

'I'm going home!' Joanna looked at him defiantly, trying hard to ignore the way his eyes roamed over her as he slowly pulled the sheets up to cover her.

'You are going to Santa Marta to your father. There you'll be close to me,' he said softly.

He just walked out, and she looked at the closed door in frightened frustration. How on earth had she got herself into this situation? Clearly she couldn't move tonight, but tomorrow she would call her mother. Her mother would collect her. That gave her pause for thought. It would take some explanation. What could she say to excuse her visit here? How could she explain? It would bring up the whole story. She lay back and smiled softly to herself, victory back in her grasp at a new thought. She would call Eileen.

Eileen came. It was Saturday and the shop was closed. They had never opened at weekends because there was always so much work to do behind the scenes, and after a few intrigued questions Eileen gave up her day to drive to London for Joanna. Although she had managed to be rather vague on the phone, Joanna knew she would have to face a serious interrogation when Eileen arrived.

For the moment she felt reasonably safe. Nora Colby brought her breakfast and told her that Mr Martella had a business appointment in the City. He wouldn't be back until well into the afternoon. By then, with a bit of luck, Eileen would be here and they would have escaped. It was quite ridiculous, Joanna mused when Nora had left. Really there was no need for this subterfuge. Why hadn't she simply told the woman she was leaving?

She looked round the luxurious bedroom as she ate her toast and drank tea. Her back was hurting like mad and she had been able to walk only with a great deal of difficulty as she had gone to the bathroom earlier. There were the stairs to negotiate and she had to get past Colby. She should just get up, dress and tell Nora quite firmly that she was now going home. The trouble was, she felt they would try to restrain her. She had wild visions of Nick Martella getting their call and storming out of an important business meeting to arrive and recapture her.

Much as she told herself that this was romantic nonsense, she could not escape the dread that lingered. The night before he had simply ignored her, her presence in his house concerning him not at all. The pain-killers had been duly administered by Nora and they had worked almost immediately; she had slept like a log.

This morning he had called in and she could see he was in no mood to console her. His brief enquiry about her state of health had been cold and impersonal.

'Feeling better?' He had stood just inside the doorway and looked at her steadily, making her feel the intruder she was.

'Yes, thank you.' As always when she was faced with him, her innermost feelings were more fearful than she liked to admit, hatred somewhat submerged. 'I can move fairly well. I intend to go home today.'

The black brows rose sceptically.

'Your intentions differ from mine. I intend to take you to Santa Marta. It's not going to be possible for three days, but I'll let your father know.'

'I won't go.' Joanna looked at him steadily and didn't even bother to raise her voice. It amused him.

'You'll learn to obey me. You might as well begin now. We leave in three days. Set your mind firmly on that.'

'This is England, Mr Martella. You can't kidnap me, take me away without my consent.'

'You're here of your own free will, as at least six witnesses can testify. What am I doing, after all? I'm merely taking you to see your father. Meanwhile you have comfort and a very respectable chaperon. If that's kidnapping, then it's a very odd way to go about it.'

She lowered her eyes to hide her thoughts, not sure even then if he could read them. The only way she was going to get out of here was by sneaking out, she could see that clearly.

'All right. I'd like to see Daddy. I'll have to get more clothes, though, and also I'll have to let my mother know.'

'The telephone is at your disposal, but I would have thought a call to your mother was unwise. How do you propose to explain your visit here?'

'I—I don't. She thinks I'm staying with a friend. In any case, I do as I like. Nobody worries about me.'

'I'm well aware of that.' Momentarily the dark eyes softened. 'Nobody has worried about you for quite a few years. I'm not blind. I think I know your family reasonably well.'

'I'm sure you don't, but, in any case, I'm not a child. At twenty-three, I live my own life.'

'Then you can live it on Santa Marta,' he rejoined promptly. 'It seems to me that you're losing your job, that nobody cares very deeply about you except your father, so what have you to lose?'

'What have I to lose?' Joanna glared up at him. 'I expect you've forgotten what you said to me at that dreadful wedding?'

Having brought the subject up, she felt her face flood with colour, and he suddenly grinned, just a bit like a satisfied tiger.

'I'm hardly likely to forget it. It's been on my mind for quite some time.'

'Have you always been insane?' Joanna enquired with sarcastic interest, but even that did nothing to anger him. His lips curved in amusement.

'Remembering your antics of yesterday, I think I can feel reasonably certain of my sanity.' He glanced at his watch, a flash of expensive gold. 'I have to go out. Rest and get better. We can discuss your problems later.'

There wouldn't be a later, Joanna mused as she waited for Eileen. After this she would keep strictly out of his way. He astonished her. He was just proposing to force her into living with him like—like an eastern potentate. It was quite unbelievable and not something she could discuss with anyone at all in case they sent her to have her head examined. Oddly enough, she hadn't dreamed last night, but it was probably the pills she had taken. She couldn't have faced him so readily this morning under normal circumstances.

She tried to time Eileen's arrival and then gingerly got dressed. When the car drew up outside she was waiting by the window, thankful that the bedroom overlooked the street. She had told Eileen to simply wait and not ring the bell, and now she crept from the room and down the stairs, every step hurting.

Joanna was in the hall when Colby appeared, and he
looked quite startled, his blank looks vanquished. The
piggy little eyes were wide open.

'Now, then, Miss Denton, we can't have this,' he
began, but Joanna had thought it all out.

'Oh, it's quite all right, Colby.' She beamed at him.
'I'm going to stay with a friend. She's here to fetch me
now. Mr Martella agrees with me that staying here is not
really suitable. People might get the wrong idea, and
he's such an important man.'

Colby puzzled it over, his brow wrinkled, and then he
looked at her with a little less suspicion.

'Maybe,' he agreed. 'All the same, I thought you had
to stay in bed. I'll get Nora.'

He nodded at her, indicating a chair in the hall. There
was the definite understanding that she was to sit there
and wait for clearance, but as soon as he went into
another room Joanna pulled the front door open and
ran down the steps, ignoring the pain in her back.

'Go, Eileen!' she gasped, sliding into the passenger-
seat and slamming the door. 'Drive off quickly, please!
They might come after me.'

'*After* you!' Eileen looked round belligerently. 'Let
them try! What the devil is this?'

'I'll tell you as we go,' Joanna said quickly. 'Just drive
off, Eileen.' They moved off with a speed that threw
Joanna back against the seat, making her wince, but at
least they were away, and she breathed a sigh of relief
as they turned at the end of the street and lost themselves in the heavy traffic of a Saturday in London.

'Now, then,' Eileen muttered grimly as they slowed to
a more sedate speed, 'let's have the gist of it.'

'Can—can I just think about it for a day or two before
I tell you?' Joanna asked nervously, and gained herself
a look similar to the one Colby had given her as she had

crept into the hall a little while ago—astonishment mixed with suspicion.

'Think about it? Listen, chum, I come all the way up here for you, get asked to take off on two wheels with you looking over your shoulder as if somebody is after you, and now I'm supposed to sit calmly and wait for some unspecified time while you think about it? No! Come clean and do it now.'

'Well, I did a very stupid thing,' Joanna confessed in embarrassment. 'I went to see somebody who's been— been pestering me. I went to tell him off and it all went hideously wrong. Er—I fell down the stairs while I was trying to get away and—and after that he said I couldn't go. I had to escape. Thanks for coming.'

'He *kidnapped* you? Listen, we'll get the police!'

'No! Oh, no. I couldn't face that,' Joanna said quickly. 'After all, I went there of my own free will. I—I just didn't know how it would end.'

'You can visit people without then being kept against your will,' Eileen stated indignantly. 'When did you go there?'

'Yesterday afternoon.' It was all beginning to feel unreal to Joanna, and Eileen looked thunderous.

'That's twenty-four hours of captivity. You can't let this go unpunished.'

'Well, I hurt my back when I was trying to get away and he—he sent for the doctor. So I had to stay all night...'

Realising it was sounding more odd with every word, Joanna faded into silence, and Eileen glanced at her, intrigued.

'He sent for the doctor? That doesn't sound too reprehensible. Let's recap, shall we? You went to London to shout at somebody who keeps pestering you. You then had to make a run for it and fell down some stairs. He sent for the doctor and kept you all night. This morning you needed to escape. Is that about it?'

Joanna nodded, thankful it wasn't her mother who was dragging this information from her. Still, her mother would not have had the interest to pry as Eileen was doing. She would probably have said, 'Really, darling!' and left it at that.

'Who is this man?' Eileen asked quietly, looking steadfastly at the road.

'Nick Martella.' Joanna tried to sound very offhand, but it came out in a whisper. Even so, Eileen braked suddenly with shock and gained herself quite a few hoots from other motorists and several mouthed comments. For once she let it pass.

'Nick Martella! Just a minute, I can't quite take this in. He doesn't have to kidnap women—they queue up.'

'I'm aware of that,' Joanna said stiffly.

There was a long and thoughtful silence, and then Eileen came right out in her usual forthright manner with the thing uppermost in her mind at the moment. 'Did you sleep with him, Jo?'

'No. It may be his intention, but it's not mine. I hate him!'

It was quite enough to silence Eileen, and they were nearly back at the manor before she acquainted Joanna with her other thoughts.

'I've decided to sell the shop to this firm Micro-Consolidates. I talked it over with Dad last night. He could do with the money back. They're getting on now, Jo, and don't have much behind them. What with the bank rate and everything, I feel I can't let him go on shouldering this burden for me. Will you move with me?'

'No, Eileen. I can't.' Joanna hadn't forgotten the unholy glee in Nick's eyes as he had assumed she would move to London. 'I agree with your move. You must do it, but I can't come. I'd better tell you why, I suppose, because you're partly in this. Martella Industries owns Micro-Consolidates. I got that from Freddy and he—Nick Martella—never denied it.'

'So this wonderful offer is because of you?' Eileen mused thoughtfully. 'What will you do, move to another place in town?'

'No. He'd only buy them out as well. He as good as said so. I'll dig a deep hole, I think, or I might kill him, or I might flee the country.'

'What is it with him?' Eileen asked in an awestricken voice. 'Does he want to marry you?'

'Oh, no, I'm to live with him. He—he's quite mad.'

'Strewth!' Eileen said nothing more, and Joanna settled back to try and ease her aching bones. What more was there to say, after all? Nobody would believe it. She wasn't sure if Eileen did. She wasn't sure if she even believed it herself. All she knew was that there was a funny feeling inside her and that Nick Martella frightened her as no one else had ever managed to do. He was a dark illusion at the back of her mind always. He controlled her dreams and wanted to control her completely. She had wondered if it was some elaborate, sick joke, but deep inside she knew it was no such thing.

Martin would be back from his honeymoon now. Her face twisted with pain as she thought of it. What had she expected, a nice card from abroad with a note, 'Wish you were here. Having a lovely time'? A year ago she could have told Martin everything and he would have punched Nick Martella on the nose. No, he wouldn't, couldn't have, her mind informed her. Nick was a good three inches taller; his lean body was a superb assembly of muscle and power. The way he stood, the way he moved assured her that he could take good care of himself. Martin was one of his minions now, in any case. How life had changed so swiftly.

When she got home her mother never even noticed she was looking pale, never even noticed her bad back. She had news, though.

'Charles phoned for you,' she said with a look of distaste. 'He needs to speak to you urgently, but of course I didn't know where you were. You would imagine from his tone that I should follow you around and hold your hand. He intends to phone you later today, so for goodness' sake stay in. I really can't have your father phoning here regularly. He's not at all suitable.'

'He's extremely well-off now,' Joanna pointed out, sitting down with great difficulty.

'Money is not everything!' Eve Calvert snapped. Which was funny, actually. After all, that was why she had married Freddy in the first place. That was what the divorce had been all about really. That was why Charles Denton could never forgive her.

Joanna settled to wait, and when her father called a cloud lifted from her heart.

'I'm going back,' he told her. 'I'm not going to the island, though, for a few weeks. I've got to go to New York to see my publisher. Come with me, Jo. I don't see enough of you. Turn your back on that place and come with me. I'm leaving in two days.'

Two days! If she could just get her back a bit more mobile, if she could just avoid answering any calls in the meantime, she would be able to sort things out with Eileen about the shop and then go—escape.

'I'll come,' she said firmly, and her father gave a whoop of delight.

'Can you get yourself to London, luggage and all? I think I'm not to darken your mother's door again, or something like that.'

'I'll manage, Daddy,' Joanna laughed. After all, she had managed once. This time, though, she would be meeting her father, and even if they should bump into Nick Martella she could cling to her father's arm and laugh into Nick's annoyed face. She was safe!

New York thrilled her. It was fast and furious, and her father obviously thrived in the atmosphere. In the two days allowed, Joanna had completed all her business. Under the circumstances, Eileen had been relieved to see her go.

'Not that I won't miss you, Joanna,' she said firmly, 'but with this problem you've got I'll feel you're safer with your father. I'll take on a girl to help and tie up this end swiftly. Of course,' she added ruefully, 'with you out of the way, they'll probably back out of the deal.'

'No, they won't,' Joanna informed her with certainty. 'I hate to have to admit it, but Nick Martella is completely trusted in the business world, according to Freddy. If he gives his word it's enough.'

'He's so far above things that he probably won't even notice,' Eileen sighed.

'He'll notice,' Joanna assured her, red-faced, and Eileen nodded thoughtfully.

'Keep in touch. I owe you plenty of money and, for another thing, I want to know how this thing works out with you and Nick Martella.'

'I shall not be seeing him again,' Joanna said sharply. 'You can send the cash, though. Send it to Hemmington Manor; Mother will post things on, but no rush. I'm not poor, and I'm staying with Daddy.'

So she was, Joanna mused happily as she stood and looked down at the busy streets. It was like looking in on a film. This was not a skyscraper block. It was a six-storey rise and her father had the penthouse apartment. Through the french doors she could go out into a roof-top garden and look down on the busy street.

He came to stand beside her as she gazed with awe at the city.

'Quite something, isn't it?' He handed her a drink and looked across at the skyline.

'I'm stunned. I wouldn't have missed this for any-thing,' Joanna said, sipping her drink and letting the hot sunshine warm her arms. 'When did you get this flat?'

'Apartment,' her father corrected. 'It's not mine. I borrow it from time to time. I'm not here often enough to own anything like this. It belongs to a friend. He lives part of the time in California,' he added when her heart almost stopped in panic. She had thought he was going to say this was Nick's apartment but obviously it wasn't, and on second thoughts, luxurious though it was, it somehow didn't have Nick's stamp on it, nor the sign of his great wealth.

Next day her father went to have lunch with his pub-lisher and Joanna went to shop, after many cautions about not taking a wrong turning. She had no intention of wandering around. She headed by taxi to the big de-partment stores and was quite content to wander round there, her mouth almost watering at the clothes on display. She was amused and quite flattered to find that her own clothes drew quite a few eyes and her English voice brought instant signs of friendship.

In the end she bought a dress, a short evening dress of midnight-blue, and, throwing caution to the winds, she bought shoes to match. By the time she left she only had enough money for her fare back and her arms were filled with parcels. She really had enjoyed herself.

Her father was relieved to see her.

'I was just going to turn out the guards,' he confessed humorously. 'I'll come with you in future. It's not worth the rise in blood-pressure while I wait.'

It gave Joanna a great lift to know he was worried about her. Her mother never wondered at all where she was. Joanna knew right then that if Nick had not now owned a house on Santa Marta she would have stayed with her father and never gone home, because it wasn't home at all. Her father was home. She could still design clothes, sell through some London outlet. She didn't need to live in England.

She had to put it out of her mind, though. Nick did have a house on Santa Marta and she could not stay here alone. She could not really stay anywhere alone, she conceded. She had been lonely for a long time, shut out partly at Hemmington Manor, a long way from her father, and now Martin was gone. Oddly enough she could think of him now without pain. Happily too, her dreams had stopped, or almost so. It was her father. She smiled at him and he gave her the usual grin.

'For that sweet look, I'll take you out tonight,' he offered. 'We'll paint the town red.'

'I've got just the dress for it,' Joanna told him excitedly. 'This is going to be a night to remember.'

CHAPTER FOUR

As IT turned out, it was a night to remember, but not
at all the sort of night Joanna had imagined. The place
was fabulous, a great nightclub with extravagant food,
dancing and a floor show, the sort of place Joanna had
never been in her life. Everything about it was expensive
and luxurious. She expected to see a film star at any
moment.

'What a place!' she murmured to her father as they
were led to their table. 'I never imagined such places
existed except in films. I'm surprised you got a table.'

'I rang up from London when you agreed to come,
and they almost laughed until I said the magic word—
Martella. Nick owns this place. People weep to get a
table here.'

It was back again, the feeling, the dark dread, but
Joanna forced it away. Nick Martella was in London.
He had no idea she was here, and even if he had he
would not bother to pursue her across New York. She
must not let him ruin her evening. With a bit of luck
she would never see him again.

Luck was not with her. When they had almost finished eating their attention was suddenly drawn to the
door into the street. It was dark outside, the bright lights
of the city taking over from the hot sun of the afternoon.
The attraction was someone about to come in and eat.
There was a sort of subdued commotion, waiters scur-
rying, the manager suddenly appearing with a beaming
smile, and shivers of cold touched Joanna's spine as the

small crowd parted and Nick Martella walked into the lights.

He's magnificent! Her mind said it all by itself, the words drumming around in her head, although her instincts shrank from him. He was in evening dress, the first time she had ever seen him like that. The radiance was there, the brilliant darkness, his eyes glittering in the lights. Someone stopped him to speak, and she saw the flash of white teeth as he answered and laughed with them.

Here, on his home ground, he looked more dangerous than ever, more threatening, and Joanna felt the sharp stab of some small pain as he turned and held out his hand to a woman who was obviously his companion for the evening. A beautiful woman, Joanna noted, glossy and almost as dark as Nick himself. The dress she wore must have cost a fortune—Joanna's experienced eye told her that—and the diamonds at her wrist were definitely real. She melted against Nick, almost swooning, and Joanna had to fight off feelings she had never in her life had to face, not even with Martin.

The deep sadness she had felt when Martin had married was nothing like this. This was turbulent, outside her understanding. She was aghast at the way she felt. She had lived inside a dark dream with this man, hated him, feared him, but drawn by a strange compulsion, and now he was here with this woman, a stranger, a new player on the stage. It was a shock as her feelings were a shock, all of it unacceptable.

To her horror, her father was delighted to see him and stood up, raising his hand to catch Nick's attention, and Joanna shuddered as the dark eyes were turned on them. He looked so dangerous, her mind told her, panicking as he turned and walked towards them. There was something about the way he moved, the way he held his head, an arrogance that had people moving out of his way.

She still had not even begun to get control of her feelings when he was at their table, shaking her father's hand and looking down at her with dark eyes.

'You know Joanna, of course?' her father was saying. She seemed to be hearing it through a haze, and Nick's reply had her eyes fixed on his.

'Of course. She was the bridesmaid to Rina and I've known her for a long time in any case. How are you, Joanna? This is a pleasant surprise.'

She didn't know what to say. He seemed to hold her in some strange bondage. Clearly he was not about to mention her excursion to his flat, and her escape seemed to have caused him no concern; he was looking at her with the sort of pleasant indifference a man of the world would show when introduced to somebody's beloved daughter.

His companion was clinging to him, sultry and satisfied like a sleek cat, as if he had been making love to her. He probably had. Joanna snapped to life and nodded to him coolly.

'I'm very well, Mr Martella. I'm taking a little holiday with my father before I plunge back into work.'

'Are you?' he drawled softly, turning then to the woman who leaned against him sensuously. 'Céline. You already know Charles. This is his daughter Joanna. She's very clever. She designs clothes. In England her reputation is growing fast.'

Céline managed a half-smile that did not disturb her glossy lips, and her eyes ran over Joanna fairly comprehensively. The message was very clear. If the dress she now wore was an example of Joanna's talents then Céline would not be beating a hasty path to her door. Joanna flushed angrily, her face hotter still when Nick gave a low, soft laugh. He had not missed the look and had not had any trouble interpreting it.

To Joanna's relief the head waiter skimmed over to say most humbly that Nick's table was, of course, ready. Her relief was short-lived.

'Perhaps we could join you here?' Nick asked her father. 'It seems a pity to use another table when we can all share this one. Did you know there is a queue in the street?'

'Is there?' Charles Denton asked wryly. 'I don't suppose you were at the head of it, Nick?'

'Only as I stepped out of the car.' Nick suddenly grinned like an impudent boy. 'I don't queue to dine in my own kitchen, Charles.'

'A bit fancy for a kitchen,' her father laughed. 'Join us, do. You don't mind, Joanna?'

Oh, yes, she minded, she minded very much, and so did Céline by the look of her, but nobody was about to snub Nick Martella. They would probably have been thrown out in a heap.

'Of course not. We'll be finished soon, surely, and then Mr Martella can have the table to himself.'

'Then it will be no fun,' he murmured, sitting next to her, having handed Céline most courteously to the other side. 'While you are here we must make the most of it. I'm sure a late night won't harm, as you have your father right beside you.' It was a subtle reminder of his plans for her, but nobody else could have imagined it.

'Wonderful! I did tell you we'd paint the town red, darling.' Her father turned on her with sparkling eyes and never even saw the panic in hers. She knew she would not stop feeling like that until Nick was right out of the room, out of the city, out of the country!

Champagne appeared as if by magic, and Nick indicated the table and the meal they had now almost finished.

'These are my guests,' he murmured as the head waiter hovered. 'We'll all take dessert together at the end and we'll have the speciality.'

The master had spoken and they were left waiting there with no ability to escape, not that her father wanted to. He and Nick seemed to be really close, and Joanna was not even expected to utter a sound, even had she been capable. Céline said nothing either—she was too busy enjoying her food. She ate like a hungry cat, Joanna observed, one of her delicate eyebrows raised as she watched the other woman. She looked up and Nick was watching her, his own food barely touched. His lips quirked with amusement and she knew he had read her rather malicious thoughts.

He stood with one fluent movement and bent over Joanna.

'Come along. We'll spin round the floor and work up an appetite for the dessert. It's famous.'

'I'm not hungry,' Joanna muttered, already on her feet whether she wanted to be or not.

'You will be for this,' her father laughed, well pleased with his exciting evening. 'It's about a hundred pounds a go.'

'But not to me,' Nick assured him, leading Joanna off. 'In any case, how do you know I didn't pop into the kitchens and make it myself?'

'You were too busy,' Céline purred, suddenly coming to life, and Joanna stiffened in the arms that already held her. There had not been a lot of subtlety in that remark, even though her father found it hilarious. Still, her father didn't know that Nick had wanted her to join the ranks of the subjugated.

She steadfastly refused to say one word even when they were out on the floor and his arms held her firmly. Nick said nothing either. He simply danced with her, nodding and exchanging greeting with other people as they passed. This was part of his empire, this glamorous place. An entirely different atmosphere had come over the room now that he was here. She could feel the excitement in the air, the way the women watched him. Their escorts didn't look too worried either, poor fools.

'So you walked into my world?' he suddenly said quietly, speaking over her head, not looking at her at all.

'*With* my father!'

'It doesn't much matter. Finally he will give you to me.'

Joanna's head shot up, her jade-green eyes furious at the arrogance. 'I'm not a pair of socks!'

He laughed and tightened his arms. 'No. You're a goal.' His dark eyes ran over her face and the clouds of golden hair. 'A golden goal. I had expected to have to pursue you across England, but now, all by yourself, you step closer.'

'I'm merely here with my father. You must be content with your feline companion,' Joanna snapped spitefully, and he looked across at Céline critically, assessing her openly.

'Céline? She's decorative, willing and very easy to please. I am not, however, content with her. I doubt if I would ever be content with a woman.' He looked down at Joanna and pulled her closer still. 'You, though, I will keep for a long time, I think.'

She started trembling. She just could not seem to stop, and to her astonishment he held her gently, changing direction and shielding her from several pairs of interested eyes.

'Stop being afraid of me,' he murmured against her hair. How could she? He was almost re-enacting her dreams, stepping nearer each time.

'I—I need to go home,' she managed in a shaky voice, gasping when she found he had danced her out on to a cool terrace.

'Not until you've tried our dessert,' he insisted quietly. 'I ordered it especially for you. I want to see your face when it comes to the table.'

Joanna looked up at him in a daze. All the danger had gone, banished at his command, and she had no idea how he had done it. The threat had drained from his voice, from his eyes, and he smiled down at her in the lights from the crowded room.

'We can't... People will...'

'Not with me,' he assured her softly. 'They will imagine I'm showing you the view from the terrace. They would not even think of interrupting.' Of course they wouldn't. They would be barred from the place and lose face with all their friends. She had heard of places like this where duchesses begged for a seat, to see and be seen.

He led her to the edge of the terrace and pointed out across gleaming water.

'The river,' he murmured. 'At night it's beautiful, glittering with city lights, calm. In the day it is not so beautiful, but then, I never come here during the day.'

Joanna just stood and looked, seeing the lights of the few boats that passed, her hot skin cooling and the panic-stricken feeling dying quietly away. She had been desperate to get away from him and now she was just willing to stand here and gaze at the quiet river. It was almost as if he had given her comfort.

'We should go back,' he said after a minute or two. 'You will be cold soon and, in any case, we don't want too many eyes on us.'

'I—I can't just walk back into there.' She was well aware that every eye would turn on them as they went back, people speculating about their time spent out here.

'Then we'll sneak in.' He opened another door and led her into a dark passage. 'Give me your hand and don't panic.' She had no alternative, and she was startled as they stepped into bright lights and delicious smells.

'*Ecco*! The kitchens!' He laughed at her astonished look and wended his way to the door amid chatter and smiling faces; she couldn't understand a word they said, but Nick was asked to try just about everything, and everyone beamed on Joanna.

'That was like a whirlwind,' she murmured as they stepped out into the lights of the restaurant. 'I couldn't understand it, but I enjoyed it.'

'They're my people.' He took her arm and looked down at her seriously.

'Surely the smart businessmen, the big business meetings ... ?'

'My work. Those in there, they're my people.' He suddenly seemed more Italian than American, and Joanna looked at him wryly.

'And the glamorous ladies?'

He never answered. His hand on her arm was warm, and he was smiling to himself, she noted.

'Your fright has gone?'

She just nodded. It had gone. Soon he would be as he had always been, a menacing force, a threat, but for one brief moment he had been different, and she couldn't understand it at all.

'I've been showing Joanna the kitchens,' Nick announced when they went back to the table, where her father waited patiently and Céline waited with obvious annoyance. 'Now we'll have the dessert.'

It just arrived as if he had transmitted some thought, and Joanna sat down abruptly because she had never seen such a concoction. Its progress across the room was greeted with gasps of awe and admiration, and Joanna suddenly realised that the lights had dimmed.

No wonder. The dessert was a masterpiece, piled high on a silver tray, ice-creams, fruits and confections, all arranged like fairy-tale mountains, syrup sliding down the icy tops, brandy aflame in a sort of moat around it. Each height was topped by a castle of wafer biscuit, and it was placed on the table at its very centre with a great deal of respect.

The chef came to serve it himself, and Joanna's eyes were as round as a child's as she watched the deft serving; the flames flickered, illuminating her entranced looks, and she suddenly looked up to see Nick watching her, flames in his eyes to match the flames on the shining silver.

She was caught up in his gaze, held for a moment that seemed timeless, and then slowly lowered back to earth as he smiled and held up his glass when the lights came on.

'To our English visitor,' he said quietly. 'Champagne and dreams, Joanna.' Of course, he meant the astonishing dessert and the chef looked mightily pleased, but Joanna was once again back in the dark spell, and this time deeper. Subtly, some of the menace had gone but, even so, there was danger in those dark eyes.

Next morning it just didn't seem real. Joanna resolutely stayed in the apartment, taking breakfast on the terrace, firmly reading the newspapers and trying to put Nick out of her mind. Her father had gone out early, and this afternoon they were going on a sightseeing trip. It didn't seem so exciting any more and she didn't have to look far for the reason. Nick excited her, the danger excited her, and last night had left her puzzled and unsure.

It had been very difficult to hate the man who had removed all her tension so unexpectedly by doing absolutely nothing at all. It had seemed that he knew she had taken as much as she could take at that moment and a cloak had been thrown around her, shielding her from the world almost.

It was fanciful and not at all likely, but then, it was fanciful to imagine that he insinuated himself into her dreams. She stared across the skyline, not really seeing anything, knowing she should go and fearing that there was really no place to go if he was determined enough to find her. Why me? Her mind asked the question, but there was no answer really.

The sightseeing was off, her father told her as he came in later. Unexpectedly he had another meeting in the afternoon.

'I can't miss it. There's something in the wind, and I wouldn't be surprised if they're thinking of filming another of my books.'

'Don't imagine you have to baby-sit me,' Joanna stated emphatically. 'I'm just hanging around.'

'And it's wonderful.' Her father reached across and hugged her. They were having lunch on the roof-garden, the roaring traffic six storeys below, and Joanna sighed contentedly.

'I could really get used to this,' she laughed.

It was once again like watching a film as they looked down, and her father's attention suddenly sharpened as a long black car drew into the kerb.

'It's Nick,' he said with pleasure.

It was. Even from here she could tell that cougar-like tread as he stepped from the car and walked towards the building. She instantly assumed he was coming here to see them, all her senses told her that, and it seemed important to chatter away if only to distract her own mind.

'Isn't it strange to see people you know from this height?'

'Nick's easily recognisable. There's something about him that other people just don't seem to have,' her father murmured. There was. It was danger.

He was walking towards the entrance, just leaving his car there, and the one or two horns that blared were certainly not reprimanding, his hand raised in acknowledgement several times. He seemed to know everybody in New York. He was like a dark prince, a prince from some world she could never hope to understand. He must be coming here. Her skin began to tingle and she sat down abruptly.

When he walked in she had pulled herself together somewhat and managed to give him a weak smile as he looked towards her. His dark brows rose ironically and he turned to her father.

'I was just passing and decided to call.' Of course, he was lying, Joanna knew that, and she carefully kept her eyes away from him. 'For today I seem to have a few free hours,' he added.

'Which is more than I have,' Charles grumbled. 'I've got to go back to another meeting. I was going to take Joanna out and about. I wanted her to get a good look at the place because I know her well enough—she won't be here for too long, much as I try to coax her.'

'Maybe I can coax her,' the dark voice suggested. 'If you're busy, why don't I take Joanna sightseeing?'

'I couldn't possibly. I—I really don't think...I wouldn't dream of troubling you...'

How easy it was to step right back into alarm and confusion. Her face flushed and her eyes turned wild, but Nick just looked at her with a very ordinary smile.

'No trouble. I'll enjoy it. Normally I'm not still long enough to enjoy the city.'

Smiles could be so different, Joanna thought uneasily. He had a collection of them: icy, menacing, scathing, seductive and now so very, very normal. She just stared at him, her own eyes changed to a deeper shade of green.

'No need to get in a dither, cherub,' her father laughed. 'It takes a weight off my conscience, and you'll be safer with Nick than with me.'

'I'm sure I won't,' she choked.

'You will,' her father asserted. 'Everybody knows Nick. If I fell down in the street people would just step over me, or on me.'

Joanna just couldn't get into the mood for good-humoured banter; too many alarm bells were ringing.

'What shall I wear?' she found herself asking Nick, and he smiled another of those smiles. This time it was kindly, like a nice big brother's, and her father beaming all over them.

'Something comfortable?' Nick suggested. He turned to her father. 'If we are out late I'll ring you.'

Late? She looked round at her father but he was still beaming, and Joanna wanted to cling on to him and shout that she was going with the wolf into the dark woods. She wanted to lock herself in her room and shout that she wasn't going anywhere at all, but her father would think she was mad, and in any case it would offend Nick, and, last of all, she wanted to go. Inside she admitted it. She wanted to go very badly indeed. He might frighten her and he almost always did, but he could set her heart racing. It was racing now.

She dressed in white jeans and a long tunic top embroidered with flowers along the hemline. It fastened on one shoulder with a concealed zip, one of Eileen's creations. She put on flat white shoes and tied her hair up into a thick pony-tail. She looked innocent, she decided. It would be quite unsuitable to try to seduce her. It was the only defence she could come up with and it must have looked good because her father suddenly became very protective and hugged her.

'Take care of her, Nick,' he said gruffly.

'I'll protect her with my life,' Nick murmured in a slightly amused voice. 'Luckily I don't think it will be necessary, however.'

Neither did Joanna. She wasn't even remotely anxious about being mugged. She was scared of stepping off into the dark depths of those glittering eyes.

It took her a while to realise that nothing was happening as the afternoon progressed. She had been tense and uneasy, but Nick was just comfortable to be with, a big brother and an amusing companion. Finally she just let her breath out in one long sigh and started to enjoy it all. He made no comment whatever, but as she risked a glance at him she saw his mouth quirk in amusement.

He must have noticed she was ready to spring away from him and take to her heels. He probably thought she was ridiculous; in fact, he had called her that when she had invaded his flat. Her face flushed, and then she saw the funny side of it and started to smile to herself too.

'I think the day can begin now,' he murmured, not looking at her at all. 'Having established my credentials, I will now show you my city.'

Joanna thought she had never enjoyed herself so much. Nick seemed to be talking endlessly, pointing things out to her. She became used to his hand on her arm, laughed at his dry humour and listened, fascinated, as they met people he knew, who seemed to range from rather elegant businessmen to construction workers who yelled down to him from scaffolding, their remarks often in Italian.

Nick slid from one language to the other with ease, and Joanna realised why he had this faint accent, sometimes not even noticeable. He was an American, but the Italian was always there, in his voice, his olive-tinted skin and his black, unnerving eyes.

Finally Nick called a halt as evening began to close around them and Joanna began to drag her feet.

'You're tired,' he said quietly, looking down at her. 'I'll call your father before we eat.'

'Are you inviting him to join us?' Joanna asked breathlessly, hoping he was not. This day had been magic. All her fears seemed to have melted, and she knew perfectly well that at any moment he could change, but for now she was almost sleepy with contentment.

'You need him here?' Nick asked softly.

'No. No, I—I was just asking, I . . .'

'Then if you do not need him I will not invite him. Any time you wish to run, say so and I will take you back.'

'I don't want to run,' Joanna said fretfully, 'and there's no need whatever to . . .'

'Then, *piccola*, we will eat without him.'

'What does that mean?' Joanna asked suspiciously.

'*Piccola*? Little, small.'

'I'm not at all little. I'm to your shoulders easily, and you're about six feet two—that makes me tall for a woman,' Joanna pointed out indignantly.

He looked down at her in amusement.

'It does not necessarily mean in size.'

'You mean I have a small mind?'

'Not at all, and you certainly have a big temper. It is an endearment,' he explained. That stopped her attacks at once.

'Oh.'

'So, honour is satisfied? Now we will eat. Italian?' he asked with a quirk to his lips, and Joanna looked abashed before breaking into smiles.

'All right. You can teach me how to eat spaghetti.'

'And let mine go cold? No way. You can have a big spoon.'

They dived across the street, dodging traffic, Joanna's hand firmly in Nick's as he dragged her along, and when they were safely at the other side he simply held on to her and she didn't try to break free.

I'm a fool, she told herself. I'm just asking for trouble. All the same, she felt wonderful.

'Cold?' Nick asked, and she paced along beside him, shaking her head and smiling up at him.

'Not at all. I'm warm as toast.'

'Ah! A funny British expression. Warm as toast. I like my toast cold.' He grinned down at her in the lights, his teeth dazzling white, and Joanna laughed back.

'Too bad,' she teased daringly.

Later, after a meal that went on and on at a small place where Nick was obviously relaxed and well liked, they walked back to where the car was parked, lingering by the river to look at the lights.

'It was three when we left your father, and now it's midnight,' Nick suddenly said softly. 'We've been together for nine hours.'

'Midnight? I didn't realise...'

'The city never sleeps,' Nick pointed out. 'It catches you up and carries you along.' He looked down at her as they leaned against the bridge. 'Nine hours and you have not run once. Do I still frighten you?'

'You never did frighten me. I just...'

With no warning she was alarmed again, more by her own accelerated heartbeats than by anything Nick had said, and his finger came to her lips, stopping the tide of defensive words.

'I frighten you. You think of me as dark and alien, violent, a threat. Have I been a threat today, Joanna?'

All she could do was shake her head, not even able to look away, and he moved closer, taking her shoulders in strong, warm hands.

'Then, for the first time, I will kiss you.'

It was time to run. Joanna knew that but she was unable to move, her eyes locked with his, her lids falling slowly as his face came closer and his lips met hers in a warm, coaxing kiss. It drained all her rising fears, and as she relaxed the kiss deepened to sensuality and she felt herself yielding in his arms. Her head began to spin, and then hands that had been stiffly against his chest crept to his shoulders without her even knowing it.

'Any fear, *piccola*?' he questioned her against her lips, and she could not answer. When she did try to answer an odd little whimper came from her throat and he scooped her closer, enfolding her completely against him.

His control was enormous. He kissed her slowly, moving away and coming back again, his lips warm and sensuous, teasing her until she gasped against his mouth and kissed him too.

He drew back then, looking down at her with un-readable eyes, his finger trailing down her flushed cheek.

'I think I'll take Cinderella home,' he murmured, and she was sure that the only heart beating wildly was hers. Nick looked indifferent. It annoyed her. Her legs were trembling but Nick was still in control of himself, no

reaction at all. She must have been a big disappointment
to him.

When he turned her away she walked silently beside
him, thankful to see the car after a few minutes.
Somehow she was humiliated by the way he had kissed
her and felt nothing, by the way he had been able to let
her go. It hadn't been like that in her dreams. In her
dreams he had crushed her, held her tightly, not wanting
to stop.

He helped her into the car and then came round to
slide in beside her, and she couldn't even dare to look
at him. He made sure she did. He never started the car.
Instead he turned her face towards him and looked at
her with burning eyes.

'Now, Joanna,' he ordered huskily. 'Now you can kiss
me back again, but this time there will be nobody to see.
We are safe here.'

He drew her towards him slowly, his eyes on her lips,
and it was just like before, the tight control, the teasing
mouth, the coaxing and the sensuality. This time, though,
when she longed to feel the hard pressure that had
haunted her dreams and when she moved further to kiss
him back his arms slid round her tightly, crushing her
against him.

His mouth was heated, demanding, his fingers moving
to tangle in her hair, and he had no trouble at all forcing
her lips apart. Sensation shot to all parts of her body as
his tongue slid into her mouth to move against the
warmth there, to search and explore, to find her own
tongue and caress it roughly.

Joanna seemed to be on fire and he fuelled it deliberately, leaning back against his door and lifting her over
him, stroking her tightly to his demanding body, as his
lips plundered hers. She had no will of her own. Soft
moans seemed to rise, unbidden, in her throat, firing

his desire more until his hand moved to her neck to touch her silken skin and she felt the zip of her tunic plunge along her body as he slid it from her shoulder to allow his lips to caress her there.

She wanted to draw back, shivering with nerves at the response he was creating inside her, but Nick murmured her name softly against her mouth, curling her against him, his hand moving over her shoulder to the swollen rise of her breast.

'Don't be afraid, *cara*,' he murmured softly, his lips caressing her creamy shoulder. 'This has been between us for a long, long time.'

It had. She knew now, and in fact she had known it for weeks. His eyes had told her this when she was still too young to even dare understand. He wanted her badly and she was almost mindless with pleasure at what he was doing to her. Her breathing was heavy and slow, as if she had just woken from a deep dream. Her breasts were tight and sharp, the remembered pain twisting inside her, only this time it was real.

Nick's body was surging against her as she lay over him, and even if he had been capable he was making no effort to disguise his desire. His hands moved feverishly to her hair, moving it from the clasp until it swung free and cascaded around them.

'Your beautiful hair,' he breathed, his teeth nipping her shoulder painfully. 'I dreamed it would flow around me as I held you. All day I've wanted you here, like this.'

His mouth sought hers impatiently as he moved her against him to allow his hand to explore further, his fingertips searching for her breast.

'More, *piccola*! Give me more,' he groaned, and then he was devouring her as his fingers found their objective and stung her rosy nipple into excited life. Joanna ignored every warning that her mind raised. She was deep inside her own dreams, the wild hot pain growing, her mouth open against his, and he was draining her of everything.

It was Nick who stopped, taking her shoulders in firm hands and lifting her away from him. It was so sudden that she couldn't believe it. Her mind could not accept that the dream was over, and she looked at him blankly, her face white as a sheet in the lights that edged the car park.

He looked away impatiently and moved to start the car, giving her no time to recover, leaving her to struggle with her zip, her hair and her trembling feelings. It was only as they were once more in traffic that she dared to glance at him and his face was tight and hard, perhaps pale, but more angry than upset.

What had she expected? She had behaved like a fool; worse, she had cheapened herself for the first time in her life. Tears came silently and she tried to dry them with her fingertips, her surreptitious actions gaining his attention after a second.

He swung into the kerb without any warning, creating havoc with the following traffic and snarling viciously at a hapless pedestrian who had to jump for his life. Then it was Joanna's turn. The blazing eyes were full on her and she shivered at his looks.

'So, you are tangled up inside, pulled apart!' he rasped. 'You think I am not? You think it doesn't cut both ways? Or did you want me to take you in a car, to claim your virginity by the river?'

Her pale cheeks flooded with colour but she was given no time to defend herself. His hand slammed down on the steering-wheel and he swore under his breath, making the colour leave her face again.

'A kiss, it was supposed to be. I should have known better. I only have to look at you to catch fire.' He turned on her heatedly. 'And why, demure little English miss? What is there about you that I can't do without?' He looked her over contemptuously. 'Pale and anxious, golden hair in an unsophisticated style, neat, simple clothes that cost very little. What makes you so special? Tell me!'

Joanna couldn't even speak. Tears would not stop coming; shock and desire, anxiety and now his rage had left her shaken and almost without coherent thought. For a minute he glared at her as tears streamed down her cheeks, and then he reached out and pulled her to him fiercely, tucking her head under his chin and staring out at the bright lights of the street.

'I want you,' he confessed tightly. 'If we had been alone in my apartment I would have taken you. I would not have been able to stop myself and surely you would not have even tried. Afterwards, and in the morning, you would have hated both of us, wanted to kill yourself.' He took out a pristine white handkerchief and eased her away, drying her eyes, sitting her up straight and starting the car again. 'It is how I am.' He shrugged angrily. 'But then, you know that already, don't you, Joanna?'

CHAPTER FIVE

NICK drove off and Joanna couldn't even begin to answer. She had been through the greatest turmoil of her life. She was shaken and feeling desperately lost, very hurt. It had all happened so quickly. A few days ago she had hated him, wanted nothing to do with him, dreaded the dreams that disturbed her nights. Now, with no warning, she was drawn into his life and quite obviously tossed out of it again.

The greatest shame was that Nick had been the one to stop. From being unwillingly pursued, she now felt that she had simply thrown herself into his arms.

After a few minutes he glanced across at her and then turned the car into a dark alley and stopped.

'Why? What are you . . . ?' She instantly panicked and he cast a look of utter irritability at her, turning on the interior light of the car and flicking down the vanity mirror.

'You want to face Charles looking like that?' She could see what he meant and she grabbed her bag, searching for her make-up and comb rather frantically. 'No hurry,' he assured her in an altogether bored voice. 'Take your time.' He leant back and looked through the open window as Joanna tried to ignore both him and the aching inside, and carefully repaired her face.

The hair took longer. It was absolutely wild, in total disarray after the way he had run his fingers through it. She tugged at it with her comb, getting more agitated by the minute as she also tried to find the clasp that had held it in place. Nick found it. After watching her for a few seconds with eyes that had suddenly become amused he reached down to the floor and handed her the clasp. She remembered then how he had tossed it there, and her face flooded with colour all over again.

'*Quante scene*!' he muttered, grinning maliciously as she turned flashing eyes on him in suspicion and embarrassment. 'What a performance,' he translated. 'I have never before had to wait while a woman put herself back together again.'

'I see,' Joanna blazed, 'normally you just walk off and leave them!'

'Normally I have not taken them apart,' he stated sardonically. 'Normally I can never summon up quite that amount of heated interest. It must be your chaste demeanour.'

He smiled sardonically, pressed a button and the windows slid up into place; then he was stepping out into the dark alley and insisting that Joanna did the same as he came round to help her.

'I'm not getting out here,' she assured him fiercely, holding on to the door. 'We'll get set upon and mugged.'

He simply hauled her out.

'I'll protect you,' he murmured drily. 'They wouldn't last long, however, if you turned that sharp tongue on them.'

'You're uncivilised!' Joanna snapped, snatching her arm away from his grasp.

'But naturally,' he agreed smoothly. 'Everything that is black and undesirable. Surely you're not surprised?'

He led her round the corner into the street, and she was being ushered into a dimly lit bar almost at once.

'Hi there, Nick!' The barman came straight up and Nick grinned at him.

'Two coffees, one brandy,' he ordered, and urged Joanna to a table at the side of the room.

There were few people there and after one look at Nick they got on with their own conversations. Joanna was still smarting from so many emotions and she glared at Nick ferociously.

'If you think I'm sitting here while you drink yourself stupid...'

'I drink white wine and nothing more,' he corrected severely, his dark eyes punishing her. 'I like to be in possession of my faculties at all times. The brandy is for you.'

'I don't need——!'

'What you need, we both know,' he stated flatly. 'However, in lieu of that you will have the brandy. I'll take you back when I think you're looking normal, so try to co-operate a little and calm down. If Charles should decide to shoot me I would have to agree that I deserve it. Colby and my other acquaintances may not take the same charitable view. Spare your father grievous bodily harm—drink your brandy and regain your composure.'

'You're like an animal!' Joanna raged quietly, and he leaned back in his chair.

'If I am,' he reminded her softly, 'then you were right there with me, melting in the same heat, eager to give me more than I was prepared to take.'

'Don't believe it,' Joanna seethed, her face glowing hotly. 'I know when to stop.'

He suddenly shot up, his strong fingers grasping her wrist painfully, his eyes burning into her.

'And did you stop with Sutton?' he grated. 'At what point did you move back and slap his hands away? Because you did not slap mine away at all!'

'Martin and I are...were...'

'Lovers?' he rasped. In a minute he would break her wrist, she was sure, and he didn't care at all who was watching, not that they were. They would look the other way if he strangled her.

'You're hurting me,' she gasped.

'Then answer me!' His eyes seemed to have caught fire, and Joanna's lips trembled.

'No,' she whispered. 'He never—never asked me, and in any case...'

'And in any case you are too shy, too demure and too afraid,' he finished for her, his voice softening. He released her wrist, and as the waiter came and placed the brandy in front of Nick he pushed it across to her. 'Drink it,' he ordered. 'You need it. Tonight you stepped into my world.' His fingers absently massaged her wrist where they had left red marks. 'It is a dark world to you, isn't it?'

Joanna looked into her coffee and never answered. Yes, it was a dark world and tonight he had proved it. She tried to ignore the fact that her heart was beating madly just at the sound of his husky voice.

He dropped her off at the apartment, coming inside to see her to the lift and going no further when she asked him not to.

'Normally I see my dates home,' he murmured wryly. 'Aren't you taken back home after a date?'

'Normally,' Joanna whispered, looking down at her shoes.

'But I am not normal?' he asked, tilting her face. His eyes ran over every inch of it, lingering on her mouth. 'You look OK,' he assured her quietly; a muscle suddenly moved at the side of his mouth and his jaw tightened. 'I hurt you, *piccola*. I'm sorry.'

Before she could answer he was gone, and she found to her astonishment that her father had gone to bed. Clearly he felt she was safe with Nick Martella. She had felt like that too until the end of the evening.

She looked ruefully at her wrist. It was slightly red, and when she undressed her shoulder still showed the marks of his passion. She shivered in the silence and slid into bed. Tonight she had stepped into the darkness, given something of herself over to Nick, and she had no real idea of what it was. It was enough to know that she didn't feel the same any more. He had stopped when she would have been incapable of it, but he had possessed her mind. The fact that she had blindly stepped towards him, had been willing to surrender when she had never even thought of that with Martin, was more frightening than anything.

Next morning Joanna was able to assure her father that she had really enjoyed herself with Nick. She was astonished at her ability to gloss over some details and make much of others. It was a very creditable performance. As usual, breakfast was on the terrace of the wonderful roof-garden, the morning papers spread beside them.

'Hmm! Gossip columns!' her father suddenly grunted. 'You never know when to believe them and when to laugh. If this isn't true, though, Nick is going to have their hides.'

'What?' At the sound of his name Joanna's heart had leapt right into her mouth, it seemed, and she tried to look amused and interested, although she knew herself that her face had flushed.

'"Nick Martella to marry,"' her father read out. 'There's a picture here. Some glossy woman.' He went silent and began to read to himself, and Joanna was silent too, stunned at the feeling that pierced her. She didn't want to hear any more. She didn't want to see the woman or see a picture of Nick. She felt as if something inside her had died, as if something had been wrenched from her violently.

'Could be truc,' her father mused. 'She's from a very high-class family. I suppose Nick needs that now.'

'Why?' It was hard not to whisper, but her father was too thoughtful to notice; his mind was elsewhere.

'It seems to me he's restless, dissatisfied. He's much more than a millionaire. What has he got to go for now but marriage, you know what I mean? He probably wants children.'

Joanna wasn't listening. She was thinking about last night, Nick's words that she would probably have hated both of them in the morning if he had taken her. Why? Because he knew this would be in the morning papers? With someone like Nick it had to be true. They dared not print it otherwise. And she remembered what Freddy had said about Nick's lowly beginnings. Maybe he needed a girl from a high-class family. Joanna was not. It was true that she lived in a stately home but it was Freddy's home. She was just an appendage, a chance addition to the family, not family at all.

The thing uppermost in her mind was how to get away, how to escape without upsetting her father, because now she knew that Nick would not come after her again. He had a fiancée, a high-class one. His days of chasing women were over. She was safe but the feeling did not fill her with happiness. Instead she felt empty.

While her father was out Nick rang and she tightened up inside as he said her name in that husky voice.

'I'm sorry. My father is out at the moment,' she informed him icily. It brought ice into his voice too.

'I rang you, not Charles. I wanted to tell you that I'm going to Chicago and then on to Japan. I'll be gone a fortnight. What are you going to do?'

'Enjoy myself. I'm going to have a nice time. Goodbye,' Joanna said coldly, preparing to put the phone down. After last night, after the things he had said, after getting himself engaged, he had the nerve to ring her up as if they were old friends. She didn't want to hear his voice, it cut into her like a knife.

'Don't put the phone down on me!' he said menacingly as if he had heard her thoughts.

'I'm so sorry,' Joanna said in her very best English voice. 'Did you want something?'

'You know damned well I want something, and you know what it is,' he grated. 'For God's sake, stop this cross-talk. Come with me!'

'What?' She had to sit down. It was so unexpected and so blatantly sexual that she felt her face flush, even though she was alone. Her hands shook so much that she had to grip the phone hard.

'Listen, Joanna, I can't come round. I just haven't got the time. I've got a business meeting and right after that my plane leaves. Everything is dovetailed to get me from one place to another with no spare time—that's how I live, that's how I work. You've got time. Pack a bag and meet me at the airport. I may not have any spare days, but I've got plenty of spare nights. It's no use pretending, because we both know what happened last night. I want you with me. You want to be with me.'

While his stupid, unsuspecting fiancée waited with bated breath? He was nothing but a fierce male animal driven by sexuality. Joanna went icily cold and it was deep in her voice.

'No. *You* listen, Mr Martella! Go on your busy way and find somebody else to fill your nights. By the time you get back I'll be a long way off. In the meantime I'll enjoy myself in safety. Perhaps the next man I meet won't either marry someone else or proposition me.'

'I'm not propositioning you! I need you!'

He was just roaring at her, and Joanna put the phone down very calmly.

Then she walked into her room, shut the door and had a good cry, rage, shame and hurt all mixed up inside. She hated him! He was uncouth, vicious, unfeeling. If she ever saw him again she would scream at him and lose all her dignity, what little she had left after last night.

When her father came back he was like a dog with two tails. They were filming his book after all and they wanted some alterations to make the film script easier.

'I'll have to go out to Santa Marta,' he said with a rueful look at her. 'I can't work here, it's too noisy. I don't suppose you'd like to come?' he asked quizzically.

'Of course I would!' Joanna grinned at him and he grabbed her in a bear-hug, swinging her round.

'I've been holding my breath all the way back in the taxi,' he confessed, 'honestly, I have. I'd better phone Nick and let him know I'm deserting New York.'

'Oh, he rang,' Joanna told him innocently. 'He's going to Chicago and then Japan. He had a business meeting first. He'll be on his way to Chicago now,' she added, not knowing whether he would be or not. She wanted to leave no clues as to her whereabouts. Let Nick think she was back in England, well out of his reach unless he wanted to alert his new fiancée.

'Poor Nick,' her father mused. 'Let's hope he's getting married. Maybe a wife will slow him down.'

Maybe a wife would get close enough to kill him, Joanna thought bitterly. She would certainly have cause to after the honeymoon, or even before. Her own chain of thought threatened to bring tears to her eyes, so she stifled it and threw herself busily into planning their departure. At least she could pretend to be happy, and

Santa Marta was beautiful. It would be unsullied by Nick too, for at least a fortnight.

By the time they went to bed the packing was done, the tickets booked for an evening flight the next day, and Joanna had planned a trip to Fifth Avenue with her father before they left. She would take all morning and buy herself something fabulous. She would reward herself for common sense. Nick was not going to ruin her days.

That night he was back in her dreams, his arms round her, his lips on hers, and when she woke in the early hours she couldn't even think of going back to sleep. She sat in front of the closed windows, looking at the city lights, and nothing she could think of would get Nick's dark face out of her mind.

Santa Marta was just as she remembered it, a little-known island in a turquoise sea, one of over a hundred, where the climate was balmy all the year round and lush tropical plants and trees stretched to the water's edge in many places. From her father's house she had an endless view of golden-white sands fringed with palms, soaring gulls wheeling endlessly on the hot air currents, but behind the house the land rose, surprisingly green and luxuriant.

The bigger islands where the tourists landed were not even in sight across a gleaming sea, and for the time being she was safe. Joanna had not been here for four years and it was like coming home. Phoebe, who had kept house for her father since he had come here, greeted her with smiles and very searching looks.

'You got a beauty here,' she at last pronounced to Charles Denton, 'a real beauty. You got a man yet?' she asked Joanna with that earthy outspokenness that was typical of the people of the island.

'No fear!' Joanna laughed, surprised how much self-discipline it took to work up any smile at all. Mention the word 'man' and Nick's face sprang into her mind. She was here to shake off the feeling, shake off the dreams. If she couldn't do it here she couldn't do it anywhere, and she had two weeks of safety.

Phoebe went off, her round face creased in smiles, and Joanna started to unpack and then flung her things down and searched for her bikini. Within minutes she was racing down the steps, out on to the sand and heading for the sea, where the waves rolled gently and broke on a clean, warm beach that stretched, empty and dazzling, for miles.

She launched her slender shape into the waves, feeling the clean, clear water close over her. This was how she would recover. The peace of the island, the warm, sunny days and the clear green sea would soothe away all memory of heated kisses and dark threat. She was away from him, safely with her father. Nothing could happen.

In the following days she rediscovered the island. Her father worked furiously, his hair tousled and his temper very uncertain, but it was all sheer bliss and gradually her face became calm, her eyes peaceful and her skin tanned.

She took over the shopping, cycling to the market on Phoebe's ancient bike and lingering among the stalls to enjoy the chatter and inspect the fruits, vegetables and the local pottery and leatherwork. It was relaxing, idyllic, a holiday she had not had for a very long time.

It was only when she went on the beach alone and saw the old fort Nick had bought and altered that she faced the fact that he was still lingering in her mind. The fort stood on a small headland, facing the sea, seeming as ready to repel intruders as it had been when it was first placed here so long ago.

The alterations were subtle, tasteful, the old cannon
still facing the sea threateningly, but the flat semicircular parade area where it stood was now a patio with
potted trees and flowers, the arch leading from it not
now an entrance to the island garrison but the way in
to a very beautiful house.

Her father had told her about it at great length, and
she longed to see it for herself. Deep inside she knew it
was for a glimpse of something that Nick had created,
planned and cherished, to let her see into that dark, surprising mind. She told herself that he was a man like
any other man and worse than most, but at night he was
still with her, forcing his way into her head, and only
her determination stopped her from fretting for him. He
was now engaged to be married, as cleanly removed as
Martin, and why should she care? She despised him.

Martin never entered her mind. Events had crowded
him out just as the trauma of her duties had held her
upright as he had married Rina Martella. Joanna tried
to remember how long it had been—three months? Four?
It was difficult to reckon it up. It seemed like another
life, another existence. She was no longer the same
person; she felt older, wiser, touched by a dark destiny,
and Nick's words came to her, cold and hard. He had
told her she should have grown out of her attachment
to Martin long ago. Now she had, but it was not the
same peaceful life. Now her life was turbulent, and she
knew that soon she would have to go back to England
and take up where she had left off.

She had been here four days—plenty of time left, but
finally time would run out. Joanna walked along the
beach and mused about it. Dared she stay and risk
things? Would Nick now let it all go? She had not gained
that impression when he had telephoned in New York.
His fiancée had not seemed to be in his mind then, only

his desires, his *needs*! Anger came back, rescuing her, and she frowned down at the silvery sand.

When she looked up, Nick was walking towards her along the beach. He was wearing white jeans and a soft blue shirt, his arms brown and strong, and her heart almost stopped. She had never expected this. It was only four days. He should be in Japan!

She had nowhere to run, nowhere to hide, and he came towards her with no expression on his face but irritation. As he came up to her he just stopped and stared at her, his mouth one bitter line, his black brows drawn together in a scowl.

He could scowl! She was suddenly not scared—she was angry again too, angry and hurt, more hurt than she had ever been in her life. How dared he drag her into his life and then let her drop? How dared he walk like a dark god into her dreams and then leave her to suffer? If she had never met him her life would have been totally different. What about his high-class fiancée now?

'Why are you here?' She couldn't think of anything else to say and she said it furiously. Nick glared at her.

'I *live* here!' He flung his arm towards the fort and then pushed his hands into his pockets, keeping pace with her as she kept on walking. He was silent, a brooding anger about him, his face tight and hard when Joanna risked a secret look across.

'I'm here because you're here,' he suddenly snarled. 'Why the hell should I be here for anything else? I'm chasing you, pursuing you, driving myself mad!'

He kicked out viciously at a pebble and sent it flying along the beach, and Joanna deliberately looked at the sea, trying to ignore him. He was not going to get her back into that dark world he ruled.

'And what happened to Japan?' she asked coldly.

'I cancelled it,' he grated, sending another pebble spinning violently. 'I'll go later. Chicago was bad enough, but I couldn't rearrange that. I had to start tracking you. Japan can wait.'

'Save yourself the trouble of tracking me. It's a sheer waste of your valuable time. I would have thought you would be using your spare minutes to stay with your fiancée,' Joanna muttered tightly.

'Don't be stupid!' He shot her a fierce, heated look and then went on walking. 'You've only got to shake hands with somebody and you're married, engaged, related or partners. I met her once,' he growled. 'She's more ridiculous than you.'

'I don't have to stay and listen to insults,' Joanna snapped.

It was hard to remain annoyed and try to freeze him. Inside her whole being was singing. It wasn't true! He wasn't getting married! He had to keep looking for her! It was hard to contain her suddenly leaping happiness. Oh, she was ridiculous all right, much more than he knew. She turned away, but he grabbed her arms and spun her round. He seemed to come to his senses then, though, and let her go, glaring at her all the same.

'Inside here you're mine!' he bit out, jabbing at his head with one brown finger. 'What's mine I own, so I can say what the hell I like!'

'Not to me,' Joanna snapped. 'It might be fine in your world, but in mine it's not fine at all. I'm not interested in dark, violent...'

From rage he was suddenly grinning. 'Honey, you've seen too many old films.'

'You fit the villain's part admirably!' Joanna's eyes were a stormy green, and Nick watched her intently, his eyes roaming over her hungrily.

'What sort of a person do you think I am?' he asked huskily.

'You're not a person at all. You're a threat!'

She just looked at him icily and walked off, but he caught her hand and swung her back, catching her in his arms when she tried to lash out at him.

'I can't keep away from you, Joanna,' he confessed thickly, looking down at her.

'What? Pale, insignificant me? Me, with shabby hair and inexpensive clothes?' Her haughty looks brought a wry smile to his hard lips.

'You, with jade-green eyes and hair like spun gold,' he corrected softly. 'You, with long, slender legs and a figure to make a man go up in flames. It makes me go up in flames. You may be smaller than me but you're killing me slowly. I'm not too good at fighting back when I'm aching inside.'

It was an unexpected confession and all Joanna could do was stare into his eyes and his arms tightened.

'I want to put you down on the sand and make love to you,' he murmured, his eyes skimming her face slowly like a long caress. 'Do you think they'd notice, all the people from the house?'

'Are there a lot of people?' Joanna was in a daze so easily. He was hypnotising her with his hands and his dark eyes, his mouth suddenly sensuous and not hard at all.

'Mmm. I brought reinforcements. Colby and Nora.' His head bent and his lips brushed her cheek, his tongue snaking out to touch her lips.

'Nick!' She tried to move but he held her fast, his hand sliding down her back, arching her towards him.

'I can't help it, Joanna.' He raised his head and looked at her. 'If I let you go, will you run?'

She bit her lips together and shook her head, and he suddenly grinned, releasing her.

'What the hell? I'd only catch you. Come on, let's walk.' He kept her hand in his and turned along the beach. 'I've got a week. Move in with me.'

Joanna snatched her hand free and sprang away from him, her hair swinging round her hot face as she glared at him.

'You're mad! Power has gone completely to your head. You haven't the faintest idea how to behave in a civilised manner!'

'I'm not civilised,' he conceded, watching her with gleaming eyes. 'I've never found it necessary. I'm not arguing with you. I *have* got power, and you already know I'm not a person. What can a threat do other than threaten?'

He made a sudden move towards her and Joanna turned and ran back the way she had come, flying over the sand as if the devil pursued. He was completely untrustworthy, she knew that for sure. The fact that he excited her was utterly irrelevant. He was too dangerous to even think about.

Nick caught her as she was almost at the trees, pushing her down on the sand and coming down with her. Before she could move he was lying over her, his body covering hers, his weight resting on his elbows as he looked down at her, smiling derisively. It was only then that she understood his duplicity. Before, they had been visible from the fort and from her father's house. Here they were secluded, only the sea and a few snowy seagulls to witness.

'Let me go!' She struggled but only briefly because each movement made her aware of the powerful body covering her own and her breath threatened to seize up in her throat. 'Let me get up, Nick!'

Not daring to move, she tried icy words, but he simply looked down at her and shook his head slowly. His fingers started to stroke back her hair, his eyes following the coaxing movement, and Joanna's skin began to grow hot.

'Nick.' Her eyes were wide open, wild, and he looked down at her, his mouth tilting in amusement.

'You're where I wanted you to be, on the sand,' he reminded her softly. 'Why should I give up an advantage? I'm uncivilised.'

His eyes began to roam over her face, and she suddenly found herself longing to touch him. She had to curl her fingers into fists to stop herself.

'Nick! Please!'

'A truce?' he enquired, still not looking further than her soft lips. 'A break in hostilities?'

'What sort of a truce?'

'Let me take you out this week while I'm here. Come and dine with me at the fort, go round the island with me, *be* with me.'

Joanna thought about it for all of a second. She dared not. Last time was too much in her mind, and she didn't trust herself any more than she trusted Nick.

'No. Let me up.'

'I can't do that,' he murmured, staring at her wryly. 'I have to threaten.'

He bent quickly and started to kiss her, hard, quick kisses that wound her up immediately, his hands clasping her head as she tried to turn away. He kissed her until she was gasping for breath and then began to kiss her all over again. Joanna still dared not move, but she fought inside, she fought the tremendous excitement, the twisting, aching pain, the desire to wind her arms round his neck, and when he lifted his head she thought she had won.

'It was a good try,' he assured her drily, looking down at her flushed face. 'Some things can't be controlled, though—like this.' His hand covered her breast, discovering the swollen, aching evidence, and she gave a soft moan as he looked deeply into her eyes. His own eyes darkened even further and he bent to caress the nipple through the thin cotton of her dress, his mouth hot and possessive.

She couldn't keep still then: she arched against him, her fingers moving into his black hair, and he moved his head sideways, resting it in the deep valley between her breasts.

'A truce, *piccola*?' he asked thickly.

'Y-yes!'

Joanna could hear her own voice trembling, and he rolled clear and stood smoothly, pulling her to her feet and steadying her as she swayed.

'You're not fair,' she whispered fretfully, and he caught her to him fiercely.

'You expect me to be fair? What's fair?' He relaxed his hold on her and looked down at her with a wry smile, the hoarse desire leaving his voice. 'I had to have a truce and, in any case, I needed that. It will have to last me for a long time. I have one week only and then I'm back in New York, and during this week, if I touch you, you'll yell that it's all unfair and call the truce off.'

'How do you know I'll even keep it?' Joanna asked, her lips twitching with amusement in spite of her aching feelings. He was like quicksilver, changing from passion to wry amusement at will. Sometimes it seemed to be for her benefit, but mostly she assumed it was for his own.

'Of course you'll keep it,' he assured her ironically. 'Unlike me, you're civilised.' He just took her hand and began to walk her home, and after a minute she couldn't help the bubble of laughter that rose inside and escaped like a tinkling bell. He was back, impossible, dangerous and utterly alien, but she was happy again, wildly happy. He glanced down at her and then pulled her against him, draping his arm around her neck.

'At least I amuse you. Is that an advantage?'

'The English have a peculiar sense of humour. Didn't you know?' Joanna asked mockingly. 'We laugh at very strange things.'

He tilted her face with the back of his wrist, giving her a brilliant sideways glance like black lightning.

'And I'm strange?'

'Weird, outlandish, bizarre and utterly abnormal.' She laughed up into his face and his eyes roamed over her sun-touched creamy skin.

'I agree with every word,' he muttered. 'I should have taken you right there on the sand. Instead I let the advantage slip away and I'm stuck with a truce instead of a girl.'

Joanna started to laugh, and he suddenly grinned, dropping a quick kiss on her parted lips; it was gentle, warm and not at all threatening, but it wiped the smile from Joanna's face because that was when her mind tried to tell her something, why she was so happy, why he walked in her dreams, why she stayed when she should run. It was something she dared not listen to.

CHAPTER SIX

LUCKILY Nick never saw Joanna's face, because her father came to the top of the steps that led down to the beach and Nick's arm left her as he waved. He went up for a drink and was immediately in a deep conversation with her father, who wanted some business information for the book, and Joanna escaped to her room without giving herself away.

She looked at her reflection in the mirror and even she could see the trembling realisation. Even her eyes had changed. It would be hard to stop him from finding out that this was more than a deep sexual attraction, because that was all Nick felt for her. One week. She would have to be constantly on guard. Then she would go back to England, find Eileen and take up her life again. It would not seem like life any more, though; more like a slow passing of days.

He invited them to the fort for dinner and, after a tussle with his conscience, her father agreed to go.

'I'm snowed under with work and I've got a deadline,' he muttered.

'My life is built around deadlines,' Nick told him drily. 'This week, however, I'm taking a holiday, and you can get down to hard work because I'm also taking Joanna out every day. I intend to show her the island.'

'She's seen it,' her father informed him with a smile at Joanna. 'She's been coming here for years, not as often as I would have liked, but she knows this island.'

'How can she? She has not seen it with me,' Nick murmured quietly. For the first time ever her father looked from one to the other of them, and his eyes were questioning.

It was all drowned in the flurry of getting ready, and Nick was waiting for them on the patio as they walked later to the fort. Joanna's pulses were racing. Somehow she felt she was stepping deeper into Nick's life, and in spite of her fears she wanted to be there.

It was a fabulous place. Nick spent some time before dinner showing them around, explaining to Joanna how he had altered it.

'Did you know it before?' he asked her when her father had declined to move another step and gone back out to the floodlit patio and his drink.

'Yes. I used to play here when I was a little girl. The cannon fascinated me. I had to be dragged from here at mealtimes. As often as not, Phoebe was out chasing me back as my father was sitting down to his lunch.'

'Then you know the look-out point above the patio?'

'Oh, yes.' She smiled up at him. 'It was my favourite place, but even I knew it was dangerous, a sheer drop to the sea, if you didn't hit the cannon.'

'It's safe now. Come and look at it.'

He led her up the stairs, wrought-iron and beautiful, along a passage where soldiers had once walked to their duties but which was now carpeted and silent, hung with crystal wall-lights, and then she was stepping into a room where the sea murmured far below, where the moonlight flooded through silken curtains that swayed in the soft night breeze.

When Joanna hesitated and hung back fearfully he took her hand, ignoring her trembling, and led her to the window, across a room that was softly lit and obviously his bedroom. He pushed the sliding windows back and she stepped out on to a now very safe stone balcony, semicircular, as the patio below, and the glitter of the sea met her gaze, miles and miles of it shimmering in the moonlight.

She could only stand entranced, and Nick stood beside her, watching her expression.

'It's beautiful, everything it should be,' she whispered, forgetting her fears. He had built a dream, a romantic dream, and this room that seemed to hang over a moonlit sea was the heart of it. For a moment she was too choked up inside to speak, and he took her arm and gently led her away, out of the room, out of danger and back to her father.

Joanna wanted to cry quite desperately because she felt she had been denied something wonderful, but Nick's dark eyes ignored her except to be most solicitous at dinner and most amused as he entertained them.

They were just leaving when Ed Colby came into the dining-room quickly.

'Phone for you, boss,' he murmured to Nick. 'New York on the line. It's that lady again.' He grinned at Nick, who sprang up immediately, a smile on his lips, and then Colby noticed Joanna. 'Oh, hello, Miss Denton.'

His face creased in what he imagined was a pleasant smile, and Joanna went hot and cold. Her father was a very smart man. He was not going to miss the fact that Colby knew her. She couldn't explain to him why she knew this hulking, odd-looking man.

'Met Miss Denton on the beach, did you?' Nick drawled, looking keenly into Colby's eyes.

'Oh, yeah. Saw her at the market too.' He was quick off the mark, she had to give him credit for that, and she smiled with relief, astounded to see a very sharp intelligence in the small bright eyes. Nick walked to the phone, very certain that he had smoothed over what could have been a very awkward moment, and Joanna slowly relaxed. This was getting more dangerous, more complicated by the minute.

When Nick rejoined them he looked pleased with himself and smiled wryly at her father.

'Sorry about the interruption,' he said smoothly. 'My grandmother on the phone.'

Her father just grinned to himself, and Joanna was utterly flabbergasted. His *grandmother*! Well, she had heard of excuses, but this one was the best yet. She glared at him and he looked most surprised. If it hadn't been for the stupid truce she would have flatly refused to go out with him the next day.

It was the beginning of the most deliriously happy week of her life—at least, it started out like that. Everything Nick did he did with expertise and with such a relish, such a zest for living that Joanna was rushed along into his days. These sparsely populated islands, on the outer edge of the tourist trade, were inhabited by warm, friendly people, ever ready to stop and gossip, and already Nick was accepted. They were rather proud of their wealthy and prominent neighbour.

One golden day dissolved into another. Nick had just asked that she be with him and at first it was all he demanded, although he commandeered all her time. From swimming in the morning, to driving round the island for lunch in some out-of-the-way place, to dinner at the fort, where her father was invariably invited, Joanna's days were filled with Nick until she could scarcely imagine life without him.

'Tonight we're going to dine out,' Nick announced one afternoon when they were all sitting on the veranda at her father's house. 'I thought we might take the boat over to one of the hotels on the bigger islands.'

'Nick likes calypso,' Charles put in as an aside to Joanna, giving Nick a sidelong grin.

'Why not? I rarely get the chance to make a fool of myself,' Nick pointed out smoothly. 'Providing that my competitors never find out, I can be myself here.'

Joanna was watching him, something she was doing with increasing fervour. He had spent the days being nothing more than a cheerful companion, deliberately silencing any other feelings that had arisen, and Joanna had been lulled into a sort of enchantment, wondering how she could ever have feared him.

'Well, I can't come,' Charles stated firmly. 'I'm teetering on the edge of completion with these alterations and I'm going to continue before I lose the thread of it. An evening of calypso would blow my mind.'

Joanna felt a shuddering excitement. It would prolong her day with Nick, and danger never entered her mind.

He had a fast motor launch. They had already taken it out several times, to swim in the many bays that indented the island, and they started out for the bigger towns across the water as the sun was sinking. Joanna sat beside Nick as the powerful boat cut through the darkening waves. The sky was wonderful at this time of day, cinnamon and vermilion, deepest yellow and glowing pink, the sinking sun laying down a trail of gold across the sea.

Joanna found it impossible to be anything other than content. She had lived these few days as if they were to be her last. She had no idea what would finally happen, but for now she simply longed to be with Nick each hour, lost when he said goodnight quietly and walked back to the fort. Tonight he would be with her for a little longer, and her eyes sparkled with excitement.

'Beautiful,' Nick murmured, and she nodded.

'The sky is always beautiful at night.'

'I never noticed the sky,' he said quietly, 'except where it touches your face, turns your hair to gold dust and tints your skin with the flush of a rose.'

Joanna looked around, startled. Poetic words were rare from Nick. If he wanted to say anything he said it briefly, concisely and often pithily. Now the words were murmured quietly, and when her eyes met his she could find nothing to say at all, not even thank you. His eyes were black in the light, sombre almost, his lips were softened and his face still. His mouth unexpectedly tilted in a smile that was very self-deprecating and his dark laughter drifted across to please her ears and bring a tingle to her skin.

'I am strange, hey? A monster with a dream.'

'Abnormal,' Joanna agreed, falling headlong into mockery to escape from the almost tangible feeling of recognition that always floated between them.

'*Ha ragione,*' he agreed. 'I should stick to my correct role.' He turned away with a smile, his dark eyes scanning the water, but Joanna did not turn away. He was beautiful to look at, a grace to his movements that was purely masculine and frighteningly arousing. He could pretend a dream, but more and more her own dreams were becoming reality.

The major islands had plenty of exclusive hotels, and Nick knew exactly where he was going. It was perfectly clear that he had been there many times before and as usual he was greeted with wide smiles, different from the sort of respect she had noticed for him in New York. Here he was simply liked, and he was very light-hearted.

It was wildly exciting. Joanna had never been to a place like this before when she had stayed here with her father. The hotel was certainly exclusive, the guests there very wealthy, and she would have perhaps felt shy and rather lost, but Nick took her hand firmly as they moved to their table at the edge of the dance-floor and then left her to simply gaze about with awe as he ordered for both of them.

It was a glittering place with just that touch of the barbarous that edged everything about the islands, a warmth that could not be kept out and a bubbling exhilaration that even insinuated itself into this up-market place.

'Got your flying nerves under control?' Nick asked wryly as she at last sat back and smiled to herself.

'I'm not nervous,' Joanna stated firmly, looking into his mocking eyes. 'I've had to face plenty of big events at Hemmington Manor.'

She wished the words back instantly. She had not even been thinking about Martin and the wedding, but obviously Nick's mind went straight to that event and his face darkened at once.

'I am once again forcing you to face a difficult situation, you mean?' he asked with tightening lips.

'I didn't mean that at all. I never even thought about... Please don't be angry!'

Joanna wanted nothing to spoil this magical night, and the plea came without thought. It had his eyes narrowing on her anxious face.

'You would care? You would care if I became angry and aloof, distant from you?'

'Yes.' She looked down at her hands, which lay clenched rather desperately together on the white cloth, and he reached out to them, his strong brown fingers enclosing hers.

'I'm trying to be civilised—you know?' She looked up and his eyes were smiling, laughing into hers, dazzling her. 'When I become a threat and not a person again you may let me know.'

'You can bank on that,' Joanna told him adamantly. 'I might storm out of here and take the boat.'

He grinned at her and enclosed her hands more warmly.

'I'll watch my step.'

Warmth seemed to be round her again and for a second they simply looked into each other's eyes until Nick took control of the situation and began to point out the people he knew or knew about, his quick, wry word-pictures bringing smiles to her face again.

It was a lovely meal, and, even before they had finished, the floor show started. There was a steel band, and later dancers joined it, coming on in brilliantly coloured costumes and giving wonderfully athletic performances. The rhythm of the calypso gradually took hold of the whole place, and as more wine was consumed the rather dauntingly wealthy guests visibly relaxed. The whole evening ended in hilarity as the beat changed and a low bar was stretched across the floor to accommodate the sinuous limbo dancers.

It was not long before there was audience participation, and Nick's white teeth showed against his dark face as he watched their antics. He was enjoying it, relaxed and almost carefree. For a while they had not spoken, and it had not even seemed necessary. This week she had grown very close to Nick and she knew it. Perhaps he knew it too.

'Are you going to have a go?' Joanna asked over the noise of the music, and he raised one black eyebrow at her, having looked at the exploits of one man in evening dress, his performance obviously influenced by several glasses of rum.

'I think not—at least, not in public. I would not want to be at such a disadvantage,' he murmured wryly as the man collapsed on to his back. 'I could escort you to the floor and you could try it, however,' he suggested.

'No!' Joanna looked at him in terror. It was not beyond him to suddenly drag her out there. His eyes had a devilish gleam.

As they went back to Santa Marta much later they were both very quiet again. The night was softened by a full moon that lit up the water and made the island visible long before they reached the small landing by the fort. As they coasted in and Nick cut the engine Joanna had a longing to ask to stay, to just sit with him until morning, watching the moonlight on the water and being beside him.

She loved him. She had fought against it for a long time, since her teens, when his dark power had frightened her, but now she had to admit it. Without Nick there was nothing at all to interest her, not one thing she could think of that would bring joy unless he was there to share it.

The realisation made her even more silent because there was no future in such thoughts, no hope at all. Nick wanted her and he was prepared to coax her for now. She had no doubt about this week. He was softening her attitude, simply waiting, and it would not last long. His nature would surface and he would demand, attack, and then it would all be over because she could never give herself without love that was returned.

'So quiet.' Nick helped her out and looked down at her in the moonlight. 'You didn't enjoy the evening?'

'I enjoyed it very much. It was wonderful!' Joanna looked up at him and smiled, but he still watched her intently.

'Wonderful? It was as good as that? It's rare to hear you enthuse so readily.'

'That's not true,' Joanna protested. 'I've enjoyed the time since—since...'

'Since we had a truce and the threat was removed,' he finished astutely. He turned her to the steps and then walked with her along the sand, taking her home. 'I'll have to give some thought to that,' he mused. 'Am I imagining it, or do you enjoy being with me when you feel no pressure, when I curb my rage and my insane desire to own you?'

She could not answer that; words sprang to her lips, but they were stifled before they could even be properly formed.

'Joanna?' When she did not reply he stopped and took her arm, turning her to face him. 'You won't admit to any enjoyment in being with me?'

'I think I already admitted that,' she said hurriedly. 'I like people, I get on easily with them. And—and nobody likes pressure, after all. Y-you're quite nice when—when...'

'Quite nice?' He tilted her face in the moonlight and looked down at her. 'How nice is that?'

Before she could speak or hedge any further his arm slid around her waist and he swung her forward, pressing her against him, his hand cupping her head. She could see the glitter of his eyes, the way he watched her, and she went on to the defensive immediately.

'You promised!'

'I promised, you irritating little green-eyed cat.' He let her go, his smile sardonic. 'Just remember that this lasts for one week only.'

'It's all I need,' Joanna informed him smartly. 'Next week you go to New York, and the week after, I go home.'

She bent to take off her sandals. The heels were sinking into the soft sand, and in any case it was a good excuse to avoid looking at him. She had wanted his arms to hold her. She longed to be kissed, caressed, but Nick must never know that.

She straightened, her sandals in her hand, and he was still there, waiting, watching.

'Why?' he asked tautly. 'Why must you go home? You are happier here. I have seen you smile this week. You have grown brown and rested. In all the time I've known you you have never smiled so much.'

'I used to smile,' she said without thought. 'I used to think I was happy.'

'With Sutton!' he bit out. 'How long will it be before you stop reminding me about him, about your lost love? How long before you grow up and forget him?'

She wanted to tell him that she could not even remember Martin's face, that another face was permanently imprinted on her mind. When Nick finally tired of chasing her she would never forget him, he would never leave her mind. As usual she defended herself.

'It's not possible to forget people to order,' she told him quietly.

He said nothing more but the night seemed suddenly darker, more cold, and Joanna was almost in tears as she saw the lights of her father's house and stepped on to firmer sand.

'I—I'll put my sandals on,' she whispered, bending and trying to get her foot into the slender straps. She was so tight with sorrow that she couldn't even begin to manage, and Nick muttered angrily beneath his breath.

He knelt down quickly, taking them from her and sliding her feet into each one, his hand on her foot. She was forced to place her hands on his shoulders to balance, and now they seemed to be frozen like that, Nick's dark eyes looking up into her face as she never moved.

He ran his hand over her ankle, his fingers against the silken skin, and suddenly the night was charged with feeling as his touch became delicate, sensuous. Joanna's mouth was dry. She was unable to move, unable to utter a word, and his hand slid further, to the back of her leg, his other hand joining the progress as he ran his fingers over the tight muscles that seemed to be locked in place, holding her fast.

Desire was in his fingertips as they continued their erotic caressing of her calves, and all the time the dark eyes held her, keeping her still, until her heart was pounding wildly, every breath an effort.

'Nick!' She gasped his name as his hands slid to her thighs, his palms flat against her suddenly heated skin, and he stood with one swift movement, reaching for her almost blindly, crushing her in his arms, his own breathing painful and uneven.

'*Dio*! How much do you think I can take of this?' he groaned. 'I want you now! *Now*!'

'Your promise——'

'Was made to be broken. Feel what you do to me. You expect me to sleep without you?'

He pressed her closer until she could feel the thrusting arousal of his body against her own. His hand slid to her hips, holding her fast as he moaned in pleasure, his blood on fire, and Joanna felt the demand of his open mouth over hers and surrendered, her cry of excitement muffled against his lips.

His tongue searched for hers, finding it and playing an erotic game before slowly exploring the warm cavities of her mouth. His hands slid over her body, heated against the silk of her dress that seemed no barrier between them, and his knee moved possessively to part her thighs.

He moved against her slowly, his hard body leaving her in no doubt of his feelings, and her own body seemed to become fluid, molten, her legs no longer capable of holding her upright.

'You want me,' he whispered against her ear, his teeth tugging painfully at the lobe. 'Tonight you're mine. One long night in my arms with no thought in your mind but me.'

And then what would follow? A lifetime of regret? What would she tell herself in the morning? He had warned her once before that she would have hated herself in the morning, and things were no different now. He pursued her because she was unattainable; tomorrow he would despise her and she would despise herself.

She pulled free, the effort of control bringing a cry to her lips that was almost desolation, and before he could recover from the surprise she flew along to the steps and into her own door. Safety, darkness and tears that lasted a long time.

It took an enormous effort to get up the next morning and when she did, when she walked out on to the veranda, where Phoebe had prepared breakfast, Joanna knew at once that something was different. For one thing, her father was not there with his head in a manuscript; he was walking back towards the house, looking thoughtful and rather uneasy.

He smiled when he saw her and then bounded up the steps to lean over and kiss her cheek.

'Pale this morning,' he observed. 'You evidently stayed out late last night. I waited up until almost two. Nick looks as bad as you do except for the expression. You look almost ill. Nick looks like thunder, the devil in him as I've never seen it. I hope it's not something to do with his visitors.'

He sat down to his breakfast, and Joanna tried hard not to ask but she had to.

'What visitors? He—he didn't say anything about visitors.'

'I think it's a surprise to him,' her father mused. 'Rina phoned early. They're staying for the next few days before going on to New York. Nick doesn't look too pleased about it, and that really surprises me. He thinks a lot of Rina.'

Joanna's heart sank like a stone. It wasn't Rina's arrival that had made Nick displeased; it was Martin. After last night Nick would be wild with anger in any case, and to then find that Martin was invading his domain would be enough to throw him into a rage to end all rages.

She was still staring at the sea, biting her lips together, when the boat shot out from the landing and sped towards the islands where tourists landed. She could see Nick at the wheel and she knew the devil really was in him this morning. At that speed he would not need to dock the boat—he would rush straight into town.

She could not eat a thing. Already she had been dreading this morning, dreading seeing Nick's anger; now she had even more to dread and she just didn't know how she was going to face it. No matter what she said, what she did, Nick would always believe that she still loved Martin. She had encouraged him to think that in the past and she knew from the things he said that it was always in his mind.

Love! She had never imagined what it was like until she had been with Nick, until her fright had subsided and allowed her to see what she should have seen years ago. It was a love with no future, merely passion for Nick and nothing else.

In a cowardly manner that was not like her at all, Joanna pleaded a headache and went back to her room. Her father made all the correct sympathetic noises, but she knew he was not really tuned in to her. He muttered that he was nearly finished and shot off himself to get on with his task.

Joanna lay on her bed and tried to go back to sleep. She had hardly slept at all last night and she was in no condition to face the day. Her only hope was that Nick would keep his guests over at the fort, but she knew it was a very slim hope indeed. Her father knew Rina, and it would be utterly bizarre if Martin didn't call after a lifetime of friendship with her.

She knew now that that was all it had been. She was in a very good position to recognise love, and her feelings for Martin now seemed very much a boy and girl affair. He had faded to being almost just an acquaintance. She would have selfishly clung to him because she had nobody else, but he had fallen in love himself and the whole thing had now evened out. If Nick had loved her perhaps they could all have been friends.

She almost managed a smile as she thought of that. No, even if he had loved her, Nick would never be a friend to someone like Martin, and he would be in too much of a jealous rage anyhow. She drifted into an exhausted sleep, not sinking deeply but remaining partly attuned to the sounds of the island. She heard the boat come back, not sounding now quite so angry, and she stirred and showered but resolutely kept inside. She was not going to risk a chance encounter with either Nick or Martin.

It was her father who took the call when it eventually came, and even he looked a little uneasy as he came to speak to Joanna.

'Dinner at the fort tonight, seven-thirty,' he said rue-fully. 'Normally I look forward to it, but there was something about Nick's voice that...' He didn't have to finish. Joanna knew what he meant. Nick was back to normal. The holiday was over as far as he was concerned. She had been counting the days, dreading the time when he would leave, but now she just wanted to hide until he went away.

Her nerves became more taut as the time approached, and she stayed in her room, preparing for the dinner as if it were some terrifying audition. She would have no defence against Nick's eyes. All she could do was try to look better than her best. She took out the Fifth Avenue dress and decided on that. It was multicoloured silk, the most expensive thing she had ever bought. Normally she wore her own designs, or Eileen's, but this dress was sheer extravagance.

It was the colour of the sunset sky; all the shades were there, the cinnamon, the vermilion, the gold and the deep, dark rose. She had a bracelet and necklace de-signed by a college friend, thick, heavy gold with a dull glitter in the light, and after days in the sun her skin was golden too. It brought a fairer shine to her hair, enlarged her eyes, and her father gasped as she came out to meet him.

'My word!' He just looked at her steadily and then smiled very knowingly. 'Nick,' he murmured, his eyes intently on her face.

'What do you mean—Nick?'

'I'm not exactly sure,' he mused, 'but one thing I do know: you're different. This week you've blossomed, like a rose unfurling. It's not me and that's for sure. It can only be Nick.'

'Too much writing can damage your brain,' Joanna warned him with a smile that didn't quite come off.

'He's dangerous,' Charles Denton said quietly. 'He's brilliant, experienced, ruthless and dangerous.'

'Your friend?' Joanna asked wryly.

'I'm a man, not a woman. Be careful, Jo. I wouldn't want to see you hurt.'

She managed a laugh, but she didn't think it fooled either of them.

Rina ran to Charles as soon as they arrived, like a lovely dark-eyed doll wanting a hug, and then she turned to Joanna and hugged her too.

'I've been wanting to come over to see you ever since we arrived, but Nick wouldn't let me. I'm so excited to see you again, Joanna.'

'Call her Jo,' a voice said, laughter at the back of it, and Joanna swung round to see Martin watching her, his eyes smiling into hers. 'Hello, Jo, love,' he said softly.

He was different too. Joanna could see it. She had once known Martin as well as she knew herself. She thought she had forgotten his face but she had not forgotten at all, and she knew it was different: his smile was different; his eyes smiled, but inside there was no smile at all. Something was wrong.

'Martin! It's so good to see you.'

For the moment she was safe, Nick was nowhere to be seen, and when Martin kissed her cheek she was very glad that only her father and Rina watched, although even they did not see the way his hand tightened on her face.

Extraordinarily, like some grotesque butler, Ed Colby appeared and dispensed drinks with a very peculiar dignity.

'Boss is on the phone,' he remarked to her father. 'It's 'is grandmother again, never stops calling.'

It seemed to amuse her father, easing some of his tension, and Rina never even noticed. Clearly she was used to Colby, who poured her a drink, held it up to the light to inspect it, and handed it to her with a frown as if it were a measured glass of milk for a child who had to have a very strict control over all she did. They all accepted that Nick had women calling him. It was normal, and Colby knew to call each one grandmother, some odd quirk of humour on his part, or Nick's.

Martin was not amused. He looked with distaste at Colby and seemed to be having great difficulty in keeping a smile on his face at all.

'Come out on to the patio and have a talk, Jo,' he suddenly said, looking at her as if it was a matter of life and death.

'Oh, no, you don't!' Rina pounced, rather desperately. 'This is a dinner party. If you two get talking about old times we'll never get a word in.'

'I've known her all my life,' Martin muttered, but he gave ground at once, and it suddenly seemed to Joanna that she had been quite skilfully cut out of things as Rina clung to Martin's arm and engaged Charles in a conversation that was just a little pointless.

It left Joanna standing alone, a rueful smile on her face. Possessive jealousy ran deep in this family, it seemed. It was probably the Italian in them. For a moment there Rina's eyes had flashed like Nick's, except that there had been panic instead of rage. She had no idea what could have gone wrong so quickly in Martin's marriage.

CHAPTER SEVEN

JOANNA was alone when Nick came in, almost isolated at the other side of the room and not one defence in sight. For a second he stopped as he saw her, as if some shock wave had hit him unexpectedly. His eyes ran over her from her shining hair to the slender brown legs that showed beneath the dress, and she heard his breath hiss out between clenched white teeth.

'For me or him?' he asked under his breath as he came up to her.

'I—i-it's just a dress.' Even to herself, her voice sounded desperate, and his eyes narrowed over her, dark and filled with anger.

'A dress for an evening out in an expensive hotel,' he grated quietly, 'and yet you did not wear it. Did you know he was coming? Did he write to you?'

'Don't be ridiculous. Martin didn't even know I was here.'

'Perhaps,' he muttered, his mouth in one straight line. 'But you knew he was here. You had time to prepare for him, to show him what he has lost.'

'Oh, please, Nick!' Joanna was on the very edge of tears, but they did nothing at all to soften him.

'Last night that is what I said deep inside. Please, Joanna, please stay with me. You ran. Will you go to him if he begs? Or will he not even have to beg?'

Joanna started to turn away but his fingers fastened round her wrist like steel.

'*Don't* turn away from me!' he bit out.

He was so angry that soon he would not care who saw, who heard, and Joanna's face flooded with colour, embarrassment sweeping over her. He let her go with a soft snarl.

'I am behaving badly,' he muttered caustically, 'like a threat!'

Colby came up with a drink, and Nick almost snatched it from him, downing it in one go.

'It ain't wine, boss,' Colby pointed out, his eyebrows raised in surprise. 'It was for Mr Denton. That was a whisky you just flattened.'

'Then get Mr Denton another one,' Nick rasped, 'me too.'

Colby went off, muttering that he supposed Nick knew what he was doing, and Nick looked down at Joanna for a minute, his eyes roaming all over her, touching her hungrily wherever they paused, and then when her knees were ready to give way under her he turned on his heel and walked away.

It was a terrible evening as far as Joanna was concerned. Nick rarely spoke to her; in fact, he rarely spoke at all, and then it was merely polite conversation. He was like a king, bored with his subjects and annoyed with the majority of them. Rina watched everything with dark eyes, and Joanna noted anxiety at the back of her looks.

She did not look like a happily married girl. She looked worried, miserable, her smiles a thin cover. Each time Martin spoke to Joanna she cut in rather desperately, clinging to his arm whenever possible, but Nick seemed to notice nothing. There was black anger in his face and he avoided Joanna's eyes all evening.

She could have burst into tears, but her father came out of his startled trance and determinedly held his own type of conversation, seeing to it that Joanna was not left out, but it was a great relief when the evening was over. Charles pleaded pressure of work and simply dragged her away.

It had not been the sort of evening they had spent so often with Nick this week. He might well have been another person and Joanna recognised him only too readily. He was back to how he had been when she had first met him, hard, ruthless and menacing, raw power barely controlled.

'Phew!' her father breathed as they escaped into the moonlit night and walked back home along the beach. 'Thank goodness that's over. Would you say that Nick was annoyed?' he added with dry humour.

'He was terrible!' Joanna took off her high heels and then walked beside her father, her face pale as she remembered last night and how she had walked beside Nick.

'Just remember this night, then, Jo,' her father advised quietly. 'Normally Nick is good company, but the devil sits deep inside him; it has done ever since I've known him. He would make life hell for a woman, and they don't last long in any case.'

'He—he's not engaged,' Joanna murmured.

'I know. He told me. His lawyers are already after the paper that printed that. They've printed things about him before and he's ignored it. For some reason he's going for the throat this time.' He glanced across at her pale face. 'It doesn't make any difference, Jo. He's surrounded by glamorous women. You saw that one, Céline. She won't even be a shadow on Nick's horizon now.'

And neither will I, Joanna mourned inside. Neither will I when he goes.

She cried when she was alone. It wasn't the first time and it wouldn't be the last with Nick. Every bit of calm and reassurance she had gained here seemed to have been drained from her last night and this evening. Nick could tear her apart, and when she realised he would be leaving the day after next she felt pulled in two directions. If she stayed near him he would destroy her, and when he left there would be nothing at all.

Next day it was like waiting for some catastrophe. Morning turned to afternoon, and there was this terrible air of listening for doom. Joanna expected Nick to do something. He was not a man to leave things alone, and there had been a whole night to brood on things. Last night he had been in a black, silent mood, like a tiger deciding upon his prey, and surely it would be her. He might hate Martin, but Martin had more protection than she had. He was married to Rina, Nick's well-loved niece, while she was nothing at all.

In the end it was Martin who acted. Joanna had never left the veranda, being too scared to risk meeting Nick away from the protection of her father, and it was with some shock that she saw Martin approaching, obviously intent on speaking to her. It had to be her—he hardly knew her father at all—and last night she had known that he wanted to get her to himself for a minute as if he had some urgent need to speak.

The manuscript was almost ready and her father was in his study, not available for visitors, and Joanna had to face this alone. Not that Martin worried her. Her worry was what Nick would do if he discovered the two of them together. He would suspect some plot, some secret assignation, and act accordingly. She wasn't sure what he would do, but it would be violent and painful.

Martin was clearly on edge. He sat down when she invited him but he was not really interested in coffee, although he accepted it as Phoebe brought it in. All the time his eyes were on Joanna, a sort of desperate look about him, and finally he stood and held out his hand.

'Come and walk on the beach.'

'I hardly think . . . I mean, what will Rina——?'

'She doesn't own my soul, for heaven's sake!' he snapped frustratedly. 'Not yet, at any rate.'

It was a strange thing to say when he was married to her, Joanna thought. Nick owned *her* soul already, and they had not even become lovers. It was apparent that she would have to stroll along the beach for a little, however, unless she wanted a childish outburst, and she had in any case no desire to act like a coy girl.

He was quiet for a while and she tried to jolly him along, reminding him about things in the past. It was all she could do because he was like a stranger to her now and she had no real idea of his problem. It was not her place now to probe into his new life.

Her laughing, nostalgic excursions seemed to make things worse, and he suddenly stopped, taking her hand and swinging her round to face him.

'I hurt you, didn't I?' he asked deeply, his grey eyes roaming over her. She used to think they were the most wonderful eyes in the world, his fair hair the most thrilling sight. Now dark eyes lived in her mind, hair like jet and a tanned olive skin. Nick's lean height was so much more arresting than Martin's smooth, tough build.

'Jo,' he murmured when she didn't answer. 'I saw your face at the wedding. Don't pretend with me. I know what it did to you.' He turned away and looked out to sea. 'It was always you, Jo, you and me together. How could I have let myself be lured into anything that took me away from you?'

'Your decision,' Joanna reminded him steadily. She didn't want to be drawn into this, to be the sounding-board for his frustrations. She had always been that and she realised it now. Martin had needed her when she had imagined she needed him, her strong, fair, grey-eyed Martin. *She* had been the strength.

'Yes. My decision. He offered me a job in London. More salary, better prospects, a chance to be part of the Martella empire. He could talk anybody into anything. He can control that temper when he wants to. He can charm you off your feet. You don't know him, Jo.'

'Did he talk you into marrying his niece?' Joanna asked quietly. Not know Nick? She knew him as she knew herself, all his passion and his rage, all his smiles and his frowns, the strength of his arms, the wonder of his kisses. He was part of her.

'He didn't have to,' Martin muttered. 'She's attractive enough, as easy to control as a child. She's also the niece of the great Nick Martella. Power, Jo! That's what I thought I had and it went to my head. Then I went in *over* my head!'

'You were there long enough to find out,' Joanna pointed out. 'Marriage is pretty drastic and final.'

This was not good. She didn't want to talk about Rina. It was distasteful, like prying into somebody's private life.

'I wanted to marry her!' he grated. 'I wanted to be part of all that wealth, all that power. I forgot you for a while. Now it's too late. She was more than willing.' His face reddened and he looked away. 'Damn it, Jo. You weren't there! I slept with her.'

'You never slept with me, so what difference did it make that I was miles away?' Joanna asked, astounded at his flustered face. He was like a boy, a selfish, spoiled boy, no more grown-up than Rina. It would have been laughable to find that somehow it was all her fault for not being there, but she didn't particularly feel like laughing.

'You would have brought me to my senses, advised me. Before I could think it was too late.'

'One night of romance, too late?' Joanna asked wryly.

'It wasn't one night,' he muttered. 'By the time I came to my senses she was pregnant. You don't walk out on anything like that, not with Nick Martella.' He scuffed his toe into the sand like a schoolboy. 'Anyway, she's a sweet enough kid, but I lost you, Jo. You were the centre of my life. I'm married, away from you.'

Joanna didn't know what to say. It was more than obvious that she had never known Martin at all. She knew now why Rina had looked miserable. Rina was woman enough to suspect that Martin was not wholly committed to this marriage.

'I'm sorry you're not happy Martin,' she began gently. 'Give it a real try. She's a nice girl. Maybe things will work out for the best after all, and——'

'They will if I can have you, Jo,' he entreated, reaching out and pulling her into his arms. 'Let me see you, Jo. Let's take up where we left off. There'll never really be anyone but you. I know you love me, and one day, when I'm free——'

'When you're approaching ninety,' an icy voice said almost in their ears.

Nick had appeared from nowhere, and Joanna remembered how far you could see on this beach. She was still in Martin's arms. She had been so startled by his words and by his actions that she had made no move at all to free herself. She had simply been standing there, looking up at him in amazement, an expression that Nick could not have seen.

He took her arm, swinging her away from Martin and thrusting her aside with such force that she almost fell headlong, and all she could see was Nick's frightening power, the dark menace, the glittering threat as he faced Martin.

'Get back to the fort!' he bit out savagely. 'You've got a wife there, and if I ever catch you even looking at another woman again I'll make you wish you'd never seen Rina!'

'Jo loves me,' Martin protested.

'Her great misfortune,' Nick rasped.

'You can't frighten me,' Martin blustered. 'Rina would die if anything happened to me. She loves me too.'

'Loves you?' Nick sneered. 'She wanted a lap-dog. I bought her one. Love is not a word that figures in the Martella vocabulary. We simply take what we want. What Rina can't take I buy for her, and you're bought. From now on you're working in Japan, well away from temptation. Don't make the mistake of trying to come back here; this is my place. Divorce Rina and you'll not even be a memory.'

'It's not true! Rina does love me!' Martin protested, and Jo could see from his face that the thought meant more to him than any power. What a fool he was. He didn't really know what he wanted.

'But you'll never know, will you?' Nick taunted cruelly.

'And what about Jo?' Martin asked. His face was pale now in view of the threats, but he was very much aware how he looked in front of Joanna. 'You can't order her about. You don't own Jo.'

'No?' Nick reached out and took her hand, pulling her forward and wrapping his arm tightly around her waist. 'You think not?'

Joanna was too shattered to resist, her trembling limbs too weak to fight, and Martin looked at her in astonishment and then contempt, his face paling more.

'So you're one of his women,' he said bitterly. 'I didn't know you at all, did I? Do you ever think about how many you share him with?'

'You're standing upright because Rina is still interested in her pet,' Nick reminded him bitingly. 'When I get back to the fort I'll expect to see you packing. You both leave tonight. Move!'

Martin left, walking along the beach, not looking back, and for a second Nick stared after him with the same menace he had used in his voice, and then he turned on Joanna with eyes like black ice, thrusting her away from him and watching her until her trembling became uncontrollable.

'Now you,' he said with sinister quiet.

'W-why did you tell him...? How could you...?'

'His ego needed deflating,' Nick rasped. 'A man who imagines two women in love with him must be floating on ego. As to Sutton, I have finished with him. He will stay with Rina until she tires of him, but he will not make any progress in my organisation. It will soon become obvious that he is merely a lap-dog. You will stay here with your father. You will not get the opportunity to take Rina's husband away. I care a great deal about my niece, enough to keep you firmly under my eye. There will be no London meeting with Sutton, no flying out to Japan to be with him.'

'I don't want to be with him!' Joanna raged, suddenly coming to life.

'Oh, I could see that,' he assured her savagely, his eyes narrowed. 'I could see how you fought to stay out of his arms, your wonderful Martin who can never be forgotten.'

'You can't force me to stay here,' Joanna snapped, using anger to cover her other feelings. Was this why Nick pursued her, to protect Rina? Was that all it was?

'Can I not?' His fingers grasped her face cruelly and he stared into her eyes. 'Did you know that your step-father lives on the edge of bankruptcy? Did you know that your mother is a hair's breadth away from being merely a housewife in a down-market suburb? Calvert's firm is teetering on the edge, ready to go under. Refuse to stay here and I will push it under. I will take Hemmington Manor and keep it for myself. The luxury that seems to be the only thing your mother requires will all disappear.'

'I don't believe you!'

'You will,' he assured her darkly. 'You think that your Freddy is more than a bumbling fool? I do not intend you to go anywhere near Sutton. Here, you cannot. He will never dare return to Santa Marta. Finally he will come to his senses if you are miles away. I intend you to be miles away.'

'You can't threaten me, you—you barbarian!'

'You will call me things like that once too often,' he muttered, pulling her against him.

The kiss he forced on her was angry and bitter, an aggressive intensity about it that made her struggle weakly. There was no escape, though. Nick's arms were like steel, and the punishing kiss continued until she thought she would faint.

Even so, Joanna felt her own body responding, yielding to him through the bitterness, and for a second his lips softened and warmed. She felt desire race through him, and then he was pushing her away contemptuously.

'Little bitch! From him to me with such ease. You stay here on the island. When I want you I take you, but right now I feel nothing but disgust.'

It wasn't true and she knew it, he knew it. Whatever his motives, he wanted her wildly, right in the middle of his raging anger. His words made her feel worthless all the same and she stared at him bitterly, the jade-green eyes awash with tears.

'I hate you!'

'Hate away,' he suggested, 'but be here all the time. Tonight I'm leaving, but remember that now I'm back to being merely a threat, now it is not your lively imagination. It's real.'

He strode off along the beach, and after a minute Joanna walked in the other direction, trying to make herself something like normal before she went back to the house. Of course, she knew that Freddy was quite out of this world. Hadn't she mused on that herself? She also knew that he was constantly up against fierce competition. That was why he had so readily agreed to anything Nick wanted, meetings at the manor, Rina's reception there.

But surely Nick could not push him under as he had threatened? She could not stay here on Santa Marta, knowing as she did that Nick might appear at any time. She would have to chance it. She went back to the house. For now she was safe with her father, although she had been anything but safe there on the beach. At this moment she *did* hate Nick, would be glad to know he had gone. What was she to him after all but a threat to Rina's happiness and an object of desire? She could see now why he had manoeuvred everyone to the manor for the wedding and reception. He had been hammering the situation in with his usual force.

It seemed to be an incredibly short time before the boat came out and headed towards the larger island. Martin was going, and it seemed that Colby was at the wheel. Rina was huddled up beside her husband and Joanna wondered what had happened when Nick had gone back to the fort. Had Rina too felt the lash of his rage? She hoped not. Rina was as vulnerable as a child,

caught between two selfish people, Nick with his rage
and Martin with his weak desire to have everything.

It was almost evening when a plane landed behind the
island, and Joanna, who had never seen that before,
looked up in enquiry.

'I expect it's come for Nick,' her father surmised as
she looked across at him. 'It's the way he usually comes.
Normally he flies it, or Colby does—they're both pilots.
He's had quite a good airstrip made behind the fort, a
couple of old fields he bought and had flattened out.
Sometimes he needs to leave in a hurry. There's always
something going off in Nick's life. Plenty of people need
his attention.'

'I didn't know he flew any small planes back and
forth,' Joanna murmured. 'He's got just about everything, hasn't he?'

'He works damned hard for it. Everything turns on
Nick and his brains.'

'He's important,' she said dully. 'It must be a change
for him when he goes home to see his people. I wonder
how they take it? His lowly beginnings will look so much
more lowly when he arrives in one of those huge cars.'

'Lowly beginnings?' Her father raised surprised eyebrows. 'It might help if I knew what you were talking
about.'

'Well, Freddy told me about Nick ages ago,' Joanna
murmured, sorry she had started this. 'He told me how
Nick was raised in the back-streets of New York.'

Charles Denton gave a great shout of laughter that
startled her, and then looked at her wryly.

'Heaven preserve me from the Freddys of this world,'
he prayed. 'If Fred Clavert had not been born into wealth
he would be selling bootlaces by now on some street
corner and, try as I might, I can't see your mother
holding a tin cup to collect the pennies.' He grinned to

himself quite maliciously; evidently the idea appealed to
him, and Joanna waited until he had had his full pleasure
out of the thought.

'So Freddy was wrong?'

'Naturally. He always is. He was born being wrong.
Nick, however, was born in Italy. His father is some sort
of nobility. I don't know what because he never talks
about it; well, not to me, anyhow. He goes back there
a lot to see him, though.'

'But—but how is it he's so well known, so many
people... I mean, rich people and poor, taxi drivers,
building workers, barmen...?' Joanna couldn't quite
take it in, and Charles smiled at her, watching her face
before he answered.

'They *like* him, love. He knows New York, it's his
city, and he never turns a blind eye to need. He was born
in Italy but he was brought up in New York. His grandmother went out there and collected him when he was
about sixteen and he's been here ever since.'

'He—he's got a grandmother?' She couldn't believe
it.

'Of course he has. You've heard him on the phone to
her,' her father reminded her.

'But I—I thought it was a woman. I thought Colby
was being diplomatic.'

'Colby is not any great shakes as a diplomat,' Charles
laughed. 'I've been there when the phone has rung for
Nick, and Colby just saunters in and says things like,
"Lisa on the phone for yer, boss." If it's Nick's grandmother he comes in pretty quick and lets Nick know.
Colby wouldn't like to cross that particular lady; she's
his favourite personality. Anyway, she's a tough
grandmother.'

'Tell me about her,' Joanna asked eagerly. She knew
nothing about Nick but she wanted to know everything,

any small thing she could store in her heart about him. 'How was it his father let her collect him?'

'I don't know. I don't know anything about his grandmother either, except that she's a very rich old lady. I saw her once—nearly. I was in the street with Nick when a car pulled up and the window slid down, and this voice said, "Nick!" He just turned as if he was programmed.

'All I saw was a hand, a very old hand, covered with rings that should have been in a bank. He bent in at the window and talked to her. I stood well back and then she sort of patted him on the head and left. Well, she didn't exactly just leave. She tapped her chauffeur on the shoulder with a cane, a black ebony cane with a silver top, and as they pulled off she called, "You're too thin, boy. Get married." Nick just stood there, grinning, looking after the car. Then he said, "My grandmother." He was so proud, as pleased as a little boy.'

So there was some softness in his life? To Joanna it meant so much. Her ideas of Nick had been built on his attitude, the hard, driving menace that seemed to surround him, his power, his wealth. To think of him as being cared for, loved, made him more human, and her eyes softened.

'Dare I ask if you're in love with Nick?' her father asked quietly, and she flushed with no hope of stopping the swift colouring in her cheeks.

'Don't be silly.'

'I hope I am being silly,' he muttered. 'I can see your flustered face, though.'

'It's embarrassment,' Joanna assured him, and he watched her for a second more before going back to his study.

'That's all right, then. You'd never survive with Nick, Jo. You're too young, too innocent. Not every woman in his life is his grandmother. And he never seems particularly interested in any of them. With Nick it would be a short, stormy life, and don't forget, he may not have been born or raised in the back-streets, but he knows them all right. He may have a wealthy grandmother, but he's built himself an empire by brains, hard work and determination. He can take care of himself anywhere. There's nothing soft about Nick.'

Joanna looked out across the sea. She knew it. She knew she would not survive with Nick. She would have to go, try to forget him. Minutes later the small plane took off and she watched it out of sight. Nick was going, and so must she, very soon. She would wait until her father was ready to go back to New York and then she would leave, go to London, find Eileen and start work again.

It seemed that with Nick gone there was nothing to do on the island. She took up where she had left off, going to the markets, wandering around, but her mind was not really on anything. Sometimes patterns and glowing colours took her eye, and then she would go back and draw them, working them into new designs, spectacular and vivid designs that caught her father's attention and gained pleased nods of approval.

Joanna wasn't one bit fooled. She knew she was good, and he was not in any case really into clothes designing. He was simply relieved that she was thinking about other things. He was hoping she would stop thinking about Nick. She wished she could.

She had brought all her things with her, her colours and pencils, paper blocks, and she was glad now. It stopped her from facing each day with dread, held off the fretting for Nick. She was designing one afternoon when the phone rang and it was Joanna who answered, almost swept off her feet by her mother's voice as soon as Eve knew who it was.

'Joanna! I've been desperate to speak to you. I had to take the risk of ringing Charles because I had no idea where you were really. Oh, Joanna, we're in so much trouble!'

It didn't sound like her mother at all, and Joanna had to spend some minutes calming her. Never in her life before had Eve appealed to her or even spoken to her as an equal.

'There's been a hostile bid for the firm,' her mother said tearfully when at last she was able to be coherent. 'I know you can't do anything, Joanna, but I had to tell somebody. So far it's not out in the open. If our friends found out... Frederick is just devastated. It would mean that we lost everything. The embarrassment of it would kill me, and there's this house. It's all tied in with the firm. I had no idea how things were. Frederick has been so stupid, and now he's behaving like someone who's going to have a heart attack.'

Joanna knew then, if she had not known before, exactly what sort of a woman her mother was. She cared for wealth and position and very little else. She was not at all concerned that Freddy would lose the home he had lived in all his life, the home his family had cherished over the generations. She was worried about embarrassment and her own future.

For herself, Joanna had not needed to pry. If there was a hostile bid she knew exactly where it was coming from. When her mother rang off, Joanna went into the study.

'Daddy? What's a hostile bid?' She tried to sound nonchalant and vague, and he looked at her over his reading spectacles, quite astounded.

'A hostile bid is a bid that is not welcome, obviously,' he told her, going back to his manuscript. It just would not do. She could fathom that out for herself.

'Er—how could it damage a firm?'

'If the firm was weak, hanging on, it would mean the bid would succeed,' he muttered, not even looking round. 'In that case, for example, the board would be out on its ear. The new owner could then do exactly as he liked, wipe the firm out and take the profits, keep it going for himself, anything.'

'What if the—the previous—er—chairman had his personal things tied up in the firm?'

Her father made a very graphic sign, drawing his finger across his throat.

'Goodbye chairman's possessions,' he said. 'He'd be selling bootlaces like Fred.' He suddenly looked round, taking an interest and grinning. 'I say! It's not Fred, is it?' He looked diabolically amused, and Joanna managed a laugh.

'Let's hope not. It was just something I've read.'

'Pity. Taken to reading my books? You might learn something. Teach you to be wary of Nick.'

He was back to work at once and Joanna escaped.

She was wary of Nick, even though she loved him. As to Freddy, she could well understand her father's attitude but she didn't have the same attitude herself. Perhaps her mother deserved this. Freddy didn't. He had always been kind to her, even though distant. He had never made her feel that she didn't have a home. She knew she could not let him sink.

She was still appalled at her mother's attitude when she had mentioned how he was taking this. If he had a heart attack then it was not going to be on Joanna's conscience. She would stay and face Nick.

Before it got dark she went along to the fort, and Nora was still there.

'I've just got to speak to Nick,' Joanna said quickly. 'There's some news he wanted to know and I must pass it on to him.'

'Well, I can give you his number, love, but he might not be there. Sometimes his meetings go on until all hours.'

Joanna tried all the same, using the phone there to keep it all from her father, safely isolated from Nora's sharp ears by a closed, heavy door, and she got to Nick—at least, she got to his apartment. His voice was a shock to her. He had only been gone for a while and yet her heart hammered at the sound of his husky tone.

'It—it's Joanna.' She was almost whispering and she knew it.

'Really? You're about to tell me that you're leaving? How nice to be informed.'

'I—I'm not leaving,' she stammered quickly. 'I'm staying.'

He was so silent that she thought he had changed his mind, and she said his name rather frantically.

'Please, Nick?'

'I'm here,' he assured her darkly. 'What exactly do you want, Joanna?'

'I know what you're doing. My mother phoned this evening. She was in a panic.'

'She would be,' he murmured sardonically. 'You expected her to stand beside her husband, laugh it off? I see no reason why he should fare better at her hands than Charles did, or you.'

'I—I can't see Freddy lose everything. It's not for my mother. Freddy doesn't deserve this. I was never close to him but he gave me a home. He never interfered. Please withdraw the bid, Nick. Don't destroy him.'

'And if I withdraw the bid, if I help him, what do I get?' he asked after listening to her and maintaining a silence for long seconds.

'You only started this to keep me here, away from Rina and Martin. You don't need Freddy's firm. Withdraw the bid and I'll stay here. I'll stay with my father and—and not go to London or anywhere.'

'Then the bid is withdrawn. I'll telephone to England now. I will also telephone your stepfather and offer my assistance. I assure you he has no idea where the bid is coming from; nobody knows that.'

'*I* know!' Tears were running down Joanna's cheeks. He wielded power like a sword, with no mercy. Why did she love him at all?

'You're crying!' Apparently he could tell, even though the tears were silent.

'What do you expect? You're utterly without mercy! I never encouraged Martin. I never intended to see him again, but you—you tear into everything and everybody.'

'Joanna!' Before she could answer another voice spoke, a voice in the same room as Nick.

'Nick, darling. Can we go now?'

He ignored the request; after all, it was just a woman.

'Joanna,' he said deeply, and she flew into a rage, her tears ignored.

'You've got what you wanted,' she shouted. 'See that you keep to the rules this time because there won't be another chance, not for Freddy nor my mother, nor Rina nor anyone else. And let me remind you what the rules are. You withdraw that bid. I stay here, but it does not mean that I have to either see you or speak to you. The next time you're here I'll lock the door and stay inside until you're gone!'

She slammed the phone down and stormed out of the house, only coming to her senses when she found herself kicking wildly at the pebbles on the beach, sending them flying as Nick had done. She was getting as bad as he was. Right now while she was so upset he would coolly lift the phone and call off the dogs, then he would go out with that woman and come back with her to his apartment to continue his hobby. She hated him!

CHAPTER EIGHT

NEXT day Joanna had a letter, posted on by her mother. It was from Eileen, and Joanna settled down to read it with a heavy heart. Eileen was free, no attachments, no heartache. Nick had touched her life too but he had touched it kindly, even if it was for all the wrong reasons. He had bought her out, offered a better position and then left Eileen alone. Why did he only bring heartache for her?

The letter was filled with enthusiasm. The place was fabulous, business very good, but she sorely missed Joanna's work. The designs were selling fast and she couldn't keep up with the demand. There had been enquiries from all over the country. She wrote,

> How about working again, Joanna? If you want to stay with your father you could work from there on a free-lance basis. I've got people to make the designs up. You could make a bigger name for yourself and make quite a packet if things go on as they are. Write and let me know what you think.

Joanna knew what she thought. She was stuck here for some time yet, and at the moment she was simply moping about, longing for Nick and dreading seeing him, her designs merely to pass time instead of a job she had trained hard for. Much more of this and she would go mad. She needed to work.

'Finished the damned thing!'

Her father appeared from his study and beamed at her, waving his manuscript, and Joanna beamed back.

'That's lucky,' she said, 'because I want your study. I'm working.'

'I'm glad, Joanna,' he said quietly, taking her shoulders in his hands and smiling down at her. 'Does this mean you're staying?'

Did she have any choice after all?

'Yes. I'm staying for now, at any rate.'

'Then take over the study, take over the house,' he suggested happily. 'I've got you back and as far as I'm concerned you can draw on the walls. You realise I've got to get this manuscript to New York? Want to come with me?'

'I'll be too busy,' Joanna said quickly. Nick was in New York and he had a nasty habit of appearing where he was least expected. In any case, she had no idea where Martin and Rina were at this particular moment. 'I'll be quite all right here with Phoebe.'

'You will. Nothing ever happens here. I don't know how long I'll be but I wouldn't leave you if I thought you were anything other than safe.' He also knew that Nick was in New York, and that was why he was happier to leave her here. They never mentioned it but it was there all right.

He left next day, and Joanna settled down to work, gathering the preliminary designs she had already done and beginning to work on them seriously. It was absorbing, and gradually she drifted back into her old habits, walking, swimming, collecting new ideas from her exotic surroundings and working sometimes late into the night. At least it kept Nick at bay, and when he stole into her dreams she awoke and walked on the moonlit beach until she had recovered. So long as she didn't see him, everything would be all right.

*   *   *

Several days later Joanna awoke with a blinding headache. She was cold, shivering in the morning heat and her skin was clammy to the touch. Getting out of bed was a great effort, and she had to rest several times before she managed to get washed and stagger out of her room.

Phoebe took one look at her and marched her back to bed.

'You got a fever, child, and small wonder, working till all hours then roaming about that beach at night. It's time your daddy came back and put a stop to it. Pity Mr Martella ain't here, he could make you take care of yourself.'

'It's a cold,' Joanna protested.

'It's a fever,' Phoebe snapped. 'You stay put, child. I gotta get the doctor.'

She was glad to be in bed and pulled the sheets up to her ears, terribly cold and shivering. The doctor came in by boat, a dark-skinned islander and very professional, and it was a fever, to Phoebe's smug satisfaction. Joanna was to stay in bed and he would come next day. He left pain-killers for her headache and told her to drink a lot.

They could call it what they liked; Joanna knew it was the flu. She felt utterly helpless, too weak to stand now, too weak to argue with Phoebe, and next day the doctor didn't come after all. At this rate she would have pneumonia, but she was too ill to care.

Some time during the following day she awoke to hear a harsh voice giving orders and laying down the law mightily. She felt too hazy to make any effort to listen. It sounded like Nick but it couldn't be, and she knew she was hallucinating. She was not. The door opened and Nick strode into the room, looking like thunder, Phoebe trotting behind him anxiously.

'She gotta stay in bed, Mr Martella, and drink a lot—the doctor said so. She won't drink an' she just sleeps and groans. It's the fever.'

'It's the flu!' Nick snapped, his hand on Joanna's hot head. 'Her throat is probably too sore to allow her to swallow anything at all. Why isn't she wrapped up warmly?'

'She keeps tossing things off.'

Nick glared at her and started to wrap Joanna up like a mummy, winding sheets over her and looking round impatiently for more.

'I'm moving her,' he rasped. 'Get her things together and put them in some sort of bag. I'll send for them.'

'Nick.' Joanna clutched at him as he lifted her out of bed, and he looked down at her reassuringly.

'It's all right. I'll get you to the fort. Nora will look after you. Where's your father?'

'The manuscript was finished. He took it to New York. I—I didn't want to go.'

'I can imagine.' He didn't look at her, he just walked out with her, and she felt dreadful, ready to cry like a child who wanted to be cuddled and was being denied comfort.

'My—my head's so bad.'

'I know,' he said more quietly, glancing at her. 'Not long now and you'll be warm, safe and comfortable.'

'You came back.' She put her head on his shoulder and he carried her out of the house and along the beach, her weight no problem.

'Luckily,' he muttered. 'You need a doctor.'

'One came, as Phoebe said. He never came back, though. He seemed to know what he was doing.'

'You'll have my doctor,' Nick informed her grimly. '*He* knows what he's doing; working for Martella Industries, he has to.'

'You can't fly him out here just for me,' Joanna croaked.

'Believe me,' Nick said sardonically, 'when I say jump, he'll jump. He's got a good job. He would fly out to me without a plane. He would flap his arms.'

'Another slave,' Joanna murmured deliriously, and he glanced down at her darkly, his eyes roaming over her flushed face.

'So why not? You refuse to be one. I have to keep the numbers up somehow. I'm judged by my retinue.' He suddenly smiled down at her. 'Be quiet. Save your strength and be good. Otherwise I'll order Colby to take care of you in place of Nora. And just realise that if you had been with me in New York you wouldn't now be in this state. I would have taken care of you.'

Right now she wanted him to take care of her. She had felt as if she was drifting away from reality with no strength, but Nick was here. He was back!

'Why did you come back?' she asked in a whisper, her throat hurting badly.

'For the same reason I always come back,' he grunted angrily, 'to see you, to touch you, to damned well hope!'

She was placed in a comfortable bed, wrapped up warmly, given aspirin and hot lemon, and before the evening a doctor arrived, as Nick had promised. He listened to her breathing, took her pulse and settled her back to sleep. He told her she had the flu.

'I knew that,' she told Nick as he came in later. She couldn't lift her head from the pillow.

'Now you know it officially.' He stood and looked down at her. 'I'll have to stay until you're better,' he muttered almost to himself. 'I'll have to put the trip to Japan off yet again. You're going to cost me a fortune.' He sounded a bit grim as he paced around the room, and she stared at him resentfully through pain-filled eyes.

'I didn't ask you to come back. I didn't ask you to rescue me. I would have been all right with Phoebe. I don't need you to be here.'

'If I leave you'll do something drastic,' he grunted. 'Don't you always? In any case, Phoebe is too old now to look after you. You're too much trouble. This is the second time you've been in bed at my place. It would be a lot less of a problem if you just moved in with me. Nora would know where she was then.'

'I'll go back as soon as I can,' Joanna said tearfully. 'I'm quite used to being in the way. My father doesn't think so, though.'

'Being in the way?' Nick walked over and stared down at her angrily. 'That's a laugh! There's Sutton wanting to care for you, your father anxious to keep you, and me hanging around like a fool. Sutton being out of the picture, it's either your father or me. Are you capable of choosing?'

'I'm not a half-wit,' Joanna said, wincing at the pain in her head. 'I can take care of myself.'

'You? A golden-haired, bewildered near-child? I've never noticed you taking care of yourself. When you're finally with me you'll realise it.'

Joanna closed her eyes tightly and he left the room and left her in peace. Right now she was so glad to be here, to know she could call out to Nora, but as soon as she was better at all she would go back to the place where she belonged, with her father.

In any case, she had to make her peace with Phoebe. Nick had almost chopped her to ribbons with his caustic tongue.

He stayed and he really did look as if he was hanging around, all his movements restless as usual. Joanna would have felt a great nuisance, but Nora took care of her, sat and talked to her when her throat began to improve, and she even got to know Colby.

He came in one morning to bring her tablets and a drink, and she smiled at him a trifle worriedly. It was a bit unnerving to have to speak to him. She knew now he had been with Nick for years, long before he had met Nora. It sounded as if Nick's grandmother had appointed him.

'Thank you—er—Colby.'

'You ain't a bit friendly,' he complained, looking at her as he got to the door. 'A real stiff English miss, not like Nora. Nick's girl ought to call me Ed.'

'I'm not Nick's girl,' Joanna said quickly, looking flustered and hot. 'I'm just here because he happened to come back and find me ill.'

'He happens to come back pretty often,' Colby drawled in that nasal tone. He walked over to the window and looked out. 'He's down there now, kicking at pebbles like a bad-tempered kid. I never seen him like this. He's tough, a big-business man, real important. You're driving him nuts.'

'I'm not doing anything at all,' Joanna protested, getting hotter by the minute.

'That's why he's going nuts,' Colby rejoined smartly. 'I know Nick, he's letting things slip for you. Should be in Japan, him and me both. You gotta come to your senses.'

'Look, Colby! Ed! You've got this all mixed up,' Joanna stated firmly, her trembling legs being securely in bed. All she got was a wry look as he ambled to the door.

'Not me. I ain't nuts. That's Nick.'

Joanna was bright red with embarrassment when he closed the door but she didn't blame Colby—Ed. It was very obvious that Nick was chasing her, and very obvious that from time to time he caught her; after all, she was here right now, and it was not the first time Colby had seen her in bed at Nick's house. She had to get back to Phoebe as soon as possible.

When Nick came back and called in to see her in his now cold-eyed way she put the whole thing to him.

'I can go back now. I won't be a lot of trouble to Phoebe. I can get up.' She still looked flustered and he eyed her narrowly.

'Nora told me this morning you were still very shaky,' he said tightly. 'You're not fit and you know it. Wanting to get me out of your sight, are you?'

'No. It—it's just that—that I shouldn't be here. People will be getting the wrong impression and...' She blushed furiously, and Nick's black brows rose, comprehension dawning in eyes that suddenly looked devilish.

'Colby's been setting you right,' he murmured, his eyes on her flaring cheeks.

'He's all mixed up,' Joanna said hotly. 'He—he called me your girl.'

'You are my girl.' He walked over and smiled at her derisively and she glared at him.

'You had no right to imply that I...'

'I don't imply, *piccola*,' he grinned, thoroughly enjoying her embarrassment. 'He's got eyes in his head. He's using his native wit.'

He suddenly bent and wrapped his arms round her, his lips seeking hers hungrily, possessive and devouring, and she had to struggle to get free.

'You'll get my germs,' she said shakily when he drew back and looked at her with amusement. He had felt her trembling response and she knew it.

'So? I want everything you've got. If you have a cold, it's mine.'

She was just staring at him, not knowing what to do or say, when the door opened after a slight tap and Colby stood there with a very bland face.

'Céline on the phone for you, boss,' he muttered, and Nick got up with a very annoyed expression on his face, striding out of the room as Colby lingered to close the door. He didn't say anything but his looks were eloquent. They said quite clearly, 'What did you expect?' What indeed? When Nick came back she pretended to be asleep and he went out, closing the door quietly but with a certain amount of suppressed violence. Whatever his real reason for chasing her, there was no doubt at all about his desire.

Joanna got up the next day, and even though she had to rest later she had finally made it to her feet. The phone never seemed to stop ringing for Nick, and he came to announce that he would have to go back to New York.

'I suppose Céline is getting restless?' Joanna murmured, trying her hand at the same scathing tone that Nick normally used.

'Well, I'll be busy,' he remarked evenly. 'Still, I like to go out at night.'

'And come back in again!' Joanna snapped. She was instantly appalled at her jealousy. Being jealous was one thing, letting Nick find out was yet another, and she stopped at once, turning away and looking at the sea.

They were on the patio, having coffee, and for a minute Nick said nothing at all. When she looked up he was staring out to sea, his face tight, and he suddenly stood and walked into the house, leaving her there without a word.

She wasn't sure why. She did know, however, that for the last couple of days he had not been in any way warm. With her illness almost over he simply wanted to get back to his business and his women. If she wasn't prepared to be one of them there were plenty who were. His every action and remark informed her of that.

Joanna made her way back to her own room, standing by the window and looking at the endless sea. Almost everything seemed to throw her into Nick's path, as if fate was determined to lead her back to him whichever way she went. And to what purpose? What was she? Someone he wanted, a passing obsession, Nick's girl—for the moment.

The other women were quite happy to be like that with him. Beautiful, sophisticated women who drifted in and out of his life, brightening his nights. Tears flooded into her eyes and began to roll silently down her face. She could never be like that. She loved him.

He came while she was crying, taking one look at her bent head and then softly closing the door. She had no idea he was there, and when he reached for her she looked round, startled and unhappy, her cheeks wet with tears.

'All right, all right,' he said huskily. 'I know, so don't even start pretending.' He turned her in his arms and cradled her against him, incredibly gentle. 'I've got to go but I want you to stay here, to let Nora look after you.' He tilted her face and began to kiss away the tears. 'I'll even leave you Colby. He can keep telling you how to behave.'

'Does he tell them all, all those women?' Joanna asked with bitter sobs. 'Does he bring them coffee in bed and give them advice?'

'Ask him!' Nick suddenly took her face in his hands, grasping it tightly. 'Ask him if I keep running after them like a fool. Ask him to name one woman who has ever been upstairs in this house other than you!'

'It doesn't matter. I'm not prying into your affairs. I don't care at all.'

'Then why are you crying? Why do you melt against me every time I touch you? *Dio*, you torture me, you torture both of us. I will give up every woman for a lifetime to have you for just one night!'

Joanna could do nothing but stare into his eyes, and he pulled her closer as if he really was tortured.

'Joanna!' He looked at her deeply, words hovering on his lips, but he never said them. Instead his lips caught hers and he lifted her against him, kissing her with a hungry passion. When she made no move to resist he swept her into his arms, his mouth still over hers as he walked to the bed and put her down, coming instantly to take her back into his arms.

'One word,' he breathed, shuddering against her. 'One word is all I need and you never say it, you never admit anything.' He looked down at her vibrantly, his eyes moving over her tear-stained face. 'You cry for me, cling to me, want me, but never the word. I know, Joanna, I *know* how you feel. Why can't you come to me?'

He sounded agonised, desperate, and when he came back to her Joanna wound her arms round his neck, her lips willingly opened below his, her body moving where he led.

'The plane, boss. It's ready.' Colby tapped at the door, and with a groan Nick moved away, his hands running through his dark hair. He looked down at her and then stood, moving to the door.

'Stay here,' he ordered softly. 'Stay here where at least I know you're safe.' He suddenly grimaced wryly. 'I used to play chess, and then there are all those women. Right now I don't have time for anything but chasing you. Pretty soon I won't even have a business. You said I tore into you. You're tearing me apart.'

He walked out, and soon after Joanna heard the plane take off. He had left her in the same turmoil that he usually did but this time she felt guilty, as if she was hurting him. Should she talk to him, tell him she could never go to him because she loved him? Could she be as open as that with Nick?

She walked back to the patio thoughtfully. No, she dared not. He would laugh at her, explain his needs and his desires and tell her the same thing he had told Martin, that the word love was not in the Martella vocabulary. The phone rang as she was passing it and she picked it up without much thought, her soft lips tightening as she heard a sultry feminine voice.

'Is Nick there? It's Annabelle.'

Fury just raced through Joanna. Minutes ago, no, seconds ago she had been contemplating putting her heart on the line, confessing everything because he had sounded hurt and lost. Now another woman was right there on the phone.

'He's already left,' she snapped. 'He'll be with you in good time for tonight.' She slammed the phone down and stood fuming.

'Was that the phone?' Colby appeared like an ugly genie and peered at her, getting himself a glare to be going on with.

'Yes. It was Annabelle this time. I told her he would be home in time for tonight.'

The nearest thing she had ever seen to a grin stretched across his face.

'She don't work nights. Annabelle is his PA. Fifty, but nice with it.' He walked out and she could hear him actually chuckling as he moved off, and Joanna's face was once again red. She remembered Nick saying at the wedding how dignified she was. Dignified! She constantly made a fool of herself when she was anywhere close to Nick. Now he was managing to have her doing the same thing when he was airborne and thinking about nothing but facts and figures. She had to get out of here.

She went to tell Nora, ignoring Ed Colby, who just stood there and listened.

'Nick wanted you to stay here,' Nora said quietly. 'You've been really ill, love. And there's nobody there to look after you.'

'I can cope,' Joanna told her. 'In any case, I must go back. Nick really told Phoebe off and I've got a few fences to mend. She's been with my father for years.'

'I can go and smooth her ruffled feathers,' Nora offered, but Joanna laughed and shook her head.

'No. I've got to go. I've got some work to do in any case.'

'I'll carry your things,' Colby said suddenly, and Joanna nodded her thanks. She hoped he wasn't going to give her any quiet advice or start any amused remarks about Nick's personal assistant.

In the event, he just walked quietly beside her, saying nothing at all until they were almost there.

'Nick's going to ring,' he cautioned her quietly. 'He's going to find out you've gone and he's going to be back here again.'

'Of course he isn't,' she snapped, glaring at him.

Glares glanced off him like water off a duck. He lived with the glares of a master. Nobody could glare like Nick.

'Don't take any bets,' he suggested.

'It's ridiculous,' Joanna fumed, wondering why she was discussing private affairs with this man. 'Why should he?'

'You're his girl.' He put her small grip by the door and turned to go. He shook his head with some sort of exasperation. 'You're a funny one. Most women would go crazy to be Nick Martella's girl. You just take off like a rabbit. It can't be because you're English—Nora's

English, and she got her head screwed on right when she was born. They must have missed a stage with you.'

He left Joanna open-mouthed. She didn't know whether to tell him he was insolent or push him down the steps. He glanced up at her as he reached the sand and she frowned as ferociously as she could.

'I expect it's because you're American,' she stated icily and obscurely.

'Yeah.' He just grinned at her and turned away, having no difficulty whatever in following her chain of thought. She had noticed before how intelligent those little eyes were. It wasn't likely that Nick would have idiots around him, except her.

Phoebe wasn't at all ruffled. She just beamed at Joanna and took her grip inside.

'I see you got over that nasty fever,' she pointed out. 'That Mrs Colby, she knows about fevers, she's been coming here for years now.'

I can't win, Joanna thought wildly. Whatever happens, I can't win. Her father phoned soon after and she grabbed the phone before Phoebe could lay a hand on it.

'I've got to go on to Florida,' he said straight away. 'Are you all right, Jo?'

'I'm fine, fine,' she assured him quickly and, to her utter fury, Phoebe leaned across and shouted into the phone,

'She's had a fever.'

'What fever?' Instantly her father was worried, and Phoebe went off, looking very righteous.

'Oh, Daddy, I had flu, that's all. Nick came back and took me to the fort. Nora looked after me,' she added hastily when he went very silent. 'I came back today.'

'Where's Nick?'

'Nick? Oh, he went back to New York.' The air seemed to be boiling across the singing lines and Joanna was worried about her father's attitude. She didn't want him coming back and messing up his schedule because of Nick's being here.

'I'm not surprised,' he said after a minute. 'He's in the middle of negotiations that are worth a small fortune. He seems to spend more time on Santa Marta than he has at his disposal.'

'Well, I'm glad he came,' Joanna said smoothly. 'It was too much for Phoebe to have to look after me.'

'Maybe I should come back?'

'If you do I'll go back to London at once,' Joanna stated firmly. 'I'm twenty-three. I don't need caring for like a child.'

'And Nick's gone?' he asked after a second's silence.

'Up, up and away,' she said cheerfully. 'I don't want either your manuscript or Nick's business on my conscience, and I've got loads of work to do, so get off to Florida and stop worrying.'

He agreed to go, and as she put the phone down Joanna bit her lips together. Her father didn't trust Nick. He was his friend but he didn't trust him. And how could he? It must have been as clear to her father as it was to Colby that Nick was chasing her. The only difference was that Colby was strictly on Nick's side. And neither of them knew the depth of his reasons.

Colby came two days later, knocking on the door and looking at her with a sort of pleading that was quite alien to him, as far as she knew. He came straight to the point as usual.

'You gotta go to New York this afternoon,' he said, pinning her with his eyes.

'I will not go to Nick!' Joanna looked outraged, but he shook his head frustratedly.

'It ain't Nick, it's her, his grandma. She says bring her here, and you gotta go. I just had her on the phone, and when she says do something I do it. She's some lady, and I do everything she says. She's arranged your plane ticket and you leave this afternoon. I take you over in the boat and I go with you and see you're OK. That's what she said. And it ain't nothing to do with Nick,' he added forcefully when Joanna looked at him with suspicion. 'He knows nothing about this. She wants to talk to you. She wants a look at Nick's girl.'

'I'm not Nick's girl.'

'Tell her that. Don't expect me to tell her. She's not to be upset. She tells me to walk on water—I do it.'

Joanna could see that he was quite prepared to take her there under his arm. She had no alternative, and she wanted very much to see Nick's grandmother in any case. This was the woman who loved him, faults and all, who patted his head as if he were a small boy. Oh, yes, she wanted to see her, and when Colby came back for her she was all ready, her overnight bag packed, and she was wearing one of her best creations.

'You look a bit thin,' Colby muttered, examining her for faults. 'Maybe she won't notice.' He grimaced at Joanna's startled look. 'She's old-fashioned. She's a real lady.'

It was like preparing for an audience with royalty, and Joanna left once again, only slightly less bemused than she had been when Nick had stormed in and rescued her.

There was no hailing of taxis, no walking and no waiting. A long dark limousine drew up as they stepped through the airport doors and a chauffeur took Joanna's bag and placed it in the back, bowing her into her seat. He very carefully refrained from looking at her and she stole a glance at Colby, who looked just a little anxious, and then they were sweeping into the busy traffic.

She almost expected a police escort. This was really extraordinary but she found herself feeling as nervous as Ed Colby, and all because of an old lady. Not any old lady, she reminded herself, Nick's grandmother, the matriarch of the Martella clan. She had been summoned to the presence and she had no idea why.

CHAPTER NINE

NERVES almost got the better of Joanna as she was ushered into a very luxurious apartment by a small, neat maid. She felt like a prisoner, the chauffeur on one side of her and Ed Colby on the other, and she knew where most of her nerves were coming from. Colby was transmitting them like radio waves. She had never seen the tough, competent man so anxious as when Nick's grandmother was mentioned.

The chauffeur left them at the door and Joanna stood waiting, looking round the drawing-room they had been shown into. It was huge, white-carpeted, draped in muted colours, very pleasing to the eye and very indicative of wealth. Colby stood like a soldier, almost at attention, and Joanna was greatly relieved as an old lady came slowly into the room. At least she was now at the stage of facing whatever it was with no further waiting.

'Thank you, Ed,' a soft, musical voice said gently. 'I really don't know what I would do without you.'

Joanna knew he bristled with pleasure, although she was not watching him; she couldn't take her eyes off Nick's grandmother. She was very old but still a strikingly beautiful woman, her ancestry all too clear in the luminous black eyes that gleamed intelligently from a pale face. Her hair was completely white but thickly piled on her head in a beautiful style that showed the arched neck that still had the poise of a girl's.

She wore a smart, expensive silk trouser suit, and Joanna noticed the ebony cane her father had mentioned and the hands covered in glittering rings. Yes, they should have been in a bank, but she couldn't think of anyone who would have the temerity to rob Nick Martella's grandmother.

'Shall I wait, ma'am?' Ed Colby asked, and the old lady smiled across at him, her eyes moving from their intent inspection of Joanna.

'No, Ed. Come back for her in about two hours. By then she will have had enough of me and this overheated apartment. I've booked her into an hotel for tonight. You can get her back to the island tomorrow before Nick finds out you've left. Our little secret, Ed.'

'Yes, ma'am.' He was red with pleasure and he literally backed out, closing the door as quietly as a whisper.

'Bring us some tea, Dinah,' Nick's grandmother said to the maid. 'The English like tea, and I'm very fond of it myself. Then you can go to the shops and leave us.'

She turned to Joanna and stood looking at her for a minute.

'So you're the girl who is making a fool of my Nick,' she said quietly. 'Come and sit down. I think I need to get to know you.'

Joanna sat and looked at her, not knowing what to say. This was not a lady to argue with. In the first place she was too dignified, and in the second place there was an amused gleam at the back of the dark eyes that made it impossible to start protesting.

'You have been ill,' she remarked, showing Joanna that she was up to date on facts. 'I know this because I tried to get in touch with Nick and I had a good idea where he would be. "Nonna," he said, "I have to stay here for a while. I can't get back." Once again he was on Santa Marta when he should have been in at least two other places. Of course, he did not enlighten me about your influenza. Ed did that. He has kept an eye

on Nick for me for years, an extraneous activity that
Nick knows nothing of.'

Joanna found herself smiling. 'Do you think Nick
needs anyone to keep an eye him?' she asked drily.

'Yes, I think so, and Ed does it admirably. Oh, I know
that Nick is tough, sometimes almost savage, but he is
the heartbeat of a business empire and when I die there
will be nobody at all to see his needs, to understand his
moods and his sombre moments. To the world he is Nick
Martella, hard, ruthless and clever. To me he is my
grandson, my dark-eyed Nick who sat at my knee and
told me his problems. He tells me them still. That is how
I know about you. You are Joanna, a golden girl from
England who thinks my Nick is a monster. I have to
know why you are making a fool of him, why he flies
to you when he should be doing so many other things.'

The maid came in with tea and Joanna had a minute
to think. She was right in the middle of Nick's territory,
facing his greatest champion. The truth seemed to be the
only way possible. She had the feeling that any equiv-
ocating would bring contempt to the dark-eyed old lady.

'Perhaps he chases me because I'm unattainable,' she
suggested quietly when they were once more alone.

'He is a brilliant businessman. He drops the unattainable.' Dark eyes roamed over her. 'Perhaps you are
necessary to his existence and therefore cannot be
abandoned?'

'He's surrounded by beautiful women,' Joanna
pointed out rather desperately, her cheeks flushing wildly.
'I doubt if anyone is necessary to Nick's existence, except
you.'

'You think a man cannot need a woman? You think
Nick does not need to come home to warm arms and
soft words?'

'He has women,' Joanna said quietly, her eyes on her clenched hands.

'Glossy dolls,' the old lady murmured scathingly. 'And fewer of those than you apparently imagine. He is wealthy and therefore pursued. You think that only a man is a hunter?' She sighed and then paused to pour tea, handing Joanna a delicate china cup. 'There have been women in his life, beautiful, mindless creatures who no doubt told him exactly what they imagined he wished to hear.' She looked up intently at Joanna. 'You are different and I have been aware of your existence for many years. He has changed his schedules for you, cancelled trips for you, spent endless time in England when it was all unnecessary. Why are you not married to my Nick?'

'He doesn't want to marry me,' Joanna said quietly. 'I'm sorry, but you've got the whole thing wrong. Nick just—just...'

'Wants you? Go ahead and speak, my dear. I am not yet a saint. I doubt if I will be pressed into that role. I too am a Martella. And if he married you, what then?'

'He wouldn't,' Joanna assured her softly. 'In any case, I would never agree, even if by some miracle he asked me. He said that the word "love" does not figure in the Martella vocabulary. I think that explains everything, don't you?'

For a few minutes the old lady looked at Joanna, and then looked out of the huge window that faced the park. It was sunny out there, hot, but inside this room there was a controlled atmosphere, no noise except the ticking of a golden clock.

'I am ninety-one,' she said after a minute. 'There are many secrets in my life, and I am very much like Nick in many ways, although I like to think I am more gentle. Today I intended to persuade you, Joanna—for Nick. But you are not what I imagined, so I will not try to bend you to my wishes. I would not succeed. Instead I will tell you a very sad story and leave you to think it out.'

She looked across at Joanna, summing her up, and then nodded to herself, and Joanna had the strangest feeling that she had passed some sort of test. She was beginning to understand why Ed Colby went in awe of this woman.

'My husband was a member of the Italian nobility,' Nick's grandmother began, 'a proud man and hard. He brought up my son to be exactly the same and I was not able to do anything but watch. I had two grandchildren, Renata and Nick, and they were destined for the same future, Nick to follow in his father's steps, but my son's wife was a charming girl, gentle, kind and loving. I felt they were safe with her and I came to America to my own relatives when my husband died.

'My son's wife died when Nick was ten years old and I think then that my son turned completely to stone. His attitude to the children was utterly cold because he could not cope with life himself. There was a great gap in their lives where a warm-hearted mother had been, but they had each other; Renata and Nick were inseparable.

'Renata was older and she married, but the two of them were very close always.' She sighed and looked at Joanna with a weary smile. 'Tragedy was not long away from us. When Rina was born, Renata also died, and Nick had lost everything in his life that was gentle. I could not get through to him. I stayed in Italy, watched his slow progress to the devil, watched him harden and grow cold, the dark eyes no longer laughing. There were unsuitable companions, rather desperate deeds, so I brought him back here to America. He visits his father often but one cannot get close to a statue.

'He was fifteen when I brought him here, almost twenty years ago. He would not leave Rina—she was all he had left of his sister. So my grandson-in-law was brought too and I built a new life for Nick and around Nick. A life to wash out the melancholy of the old country. It has worked until now. For the past six years he has been restless, impatient and now—miserable. He first saw you six years ago. I can only draw my own conclusions.'

She said nothing more. Her eyes were again seeing only the green park and a land far away, unhappy times that clearly lived with her, and Joanna could not even begin to express her feelings of sympathy. She was sure they would not be welcome. Here was a woman who took life by the chin and altered it, a woman who had lived with sorrow and risen over it.

'I expect you will think that he is a man now and more than capable of casting off the past?' she murmured quietly. 'Who knows, though, what the past does to us?'

'Many things,' Joanna agreed softly. Hadn't it done things to her, made her feel rootless, torn between her father and a life she had been forced to live in England? 'I understand.'

'Yes. You would.' The brilliant old eyes looked at her closely. 'You tell me that Nick says the word love does not appear in our vocabulary. Perhaps for him it is because it appeared too deeply and was torn away, each time because of a woman who left him without being able to stay. You have a choice, Joanna. You are able to stay.'

'For how long?' Joanna asked with soft bitterness. 'Nick chases me for a lot of reasons.' She blushed. 'I wouldn't be telling anyone else about this.'

'Then I'm flattered, my dear.' The old lady smiled, her rather regal face softened. 'Yes, I can believe that he does. How do you know that this will not last for a whole lifetime?'

'It isn't love,' Joanna pointed out quietly.

'Perhaps it is. Perhaps it is Nick's kind of love. Do you love him?'

Joanna looked at her warily and the old lady laughed, a quiet, dark laugh, very much like Nick's.

'I am the keeper of many secrets, Joanna. Nick tells me most things but I do not tell him every small secret of my own. What use would I be to him if I did?'

'Yes. I love him,' Joanna confessed. 'For a long time I was afraid of him, thought I hated him. He took away the man I thought I loved, and I imagined I'd never recover. How stupid it would have been. Now I can't even remember Martin's face.'

'He married Rina? Yes, I have met him, quite recently. I was not able to attend the wedding. It was so far away.' She made a wry face. 'He is not like my Nick and certainly not the man for you. In time Rina will learn to handle him and I think she will interest him more as she grows older and wiser.' She stood quite vigorously and smiled down at Joanna. 'We have exchanged secrets and now I think I know you. I must leave the rest to you. Think with your heart, Joanna. At the moment I can only conclude that Nick is doing precisely that. Certainly he is not using much common sense. Now I am going to show you my apartment and my treasures. I do not often get the chance to show off. At my age one enjoys luxury, and I have plenty of it.'

When later Colby came for her he was like a wary cat and obviously astonished to see Joanna in deep discussion with Nick's grandmother about clothes design. The time had flown, and on the coffee-table were sketches of clothes that would suit a very regal lady. She was deeply interested. Nick's grandmother had not in any way dropped her hold on either life or vanity. She actually came to the door with them, still talking, ordering Joanna to complete the designs and get them made up for her in London.

Colby was filled with awe. He kept silent until he had taken Joanna right to the door of her hotel room, an order clearly given to him beforehand. She had the door open when he suddenly grasped her arm with strong blunt fingers.

'What did she say?' he asked eagerly, and Joanna smiled at him with a great deal of mischievous pleasure.

'Mind your own business,' she said tartly. 'I'll see you tomorrow.' She closed the door in his irritated face and suddenly felt like singing.

How true was it? Did Nick want her for a lifetime? Was it the argument of an old lady who loved him and nothing more, or did Nick really need her? He had said more than once that he did. Rina would learn to handle Martin, his grandmother had said. Would she learn to handle Nick? How did one handle somebody like Nick? She could only love him, she had no other skills, no brilliance to match his, none of the weary knowledge of the world that Nick possessed.

But he was magic to her, a dark dream that trembled on the edge of reality, and his grandmother had drawn her in more deeply still She wanted to see him, to run to him, but she must go warily or it would all slip from her fingers and Nick would go on his dark, silent way, leaving her forever lost.

When she got back to Santa Marta she started work immediately, her mind now not only on clothes for women of her own age and younger. She had met a very young old lady and it had broadened her outlook. Looking back at it, she felt she had been with a friend, but maybe that was just because she loved Nick.

He did not come. Her father rang to check up on her safety but she did not tell him about her trip. It was a secret. Only Colby knew, and now when she went to have coffee with Nora he joined them, his little eyes amused when they met hers. Nick's tough manservant was now a co-conspirator and evidently it pleased him.

She listened for the plane but it never came. Maybe he was in Japan, maybe still in New York or even in England. He never rang, never came, and after a while her hopes began to die, the singing inside stopped and she felt once again unhappy.

She was locked in Nick's arms, her legs entwined with his, and he was kissing her passionately. He was not angry, not threatening at all. Everything about him was loving, and desire raged through both of them like white heat.

'Nick! Nick!'

The sound of her own voice woke Joanna and she sat up in bed, her heart pounding madly, her eyes on the moonlight that drifted into the room. The dream again. She was hot and breathless, her body still attuned to Nick's arms, and she tried to fight it off as she got out of bed and went to the window.

How long was this going to go on? How much more of it could she stand? It would have been better to get away from here where everything reminded her of him. She was trapped now more than ever, unable to escape because she could not leave Nick. She could still feel his hands on her skin, the dream hanging around like reality, and she let herself out of the house, not stopping to dress, doing what she had done many times before, escaping on to the deserted beach.

She had not bothered with sandals. The sand was still warm from the day's heat, and she walked close to the sea, letting the cool breeze drift over her skin through the thin cotton nightie, trying to think of nothing at all. She could not leave her body behind. It reminded her as it always did. She was aching inside, longing for Nick's arms.

A patch of white on the sand attracted her attention and for the first time ever she had misgivings about being here alone in the night. Perhaps it was something washed up by the sea? It was not very likely. It was well back from the water on dry sand and she became very cautious as she approached, her senses alert in case she had to run, very much aware that she wore only a short cotton nightie. It was perfectly decent but it made her feel vulnerable. She had never before given even a thought to being here alone like this. Nobody came on this beach.

It was a towel. She could see that even before she came close, and she walked forward very slowly, mystified by its appearance. She had certainly not left it there earlier, and for days she had not seen a soul apart from Phoebe and the Colbys.

The sound of movement in the sea had her spinning round with thumping heart, and Nick was wading ashore, his body gleaming in the moonlight, dark, brief swimming trunks covering him, his hair wet and black, his eyes fixed on her vibrantly.

'You—you're in New York.' Joanna was transfixed, held fast by his eyes and his unexpected appearance. It was almost as if she had conjured him up out of her own head, and her body began to slide back into her dream, her breasts tingling, everything inside her warm, yielding.

'I arrived about an hour ago.' He came towards her from the sea, his eyes never leaving hers. 'I left as soon as my last meeting for the day was over. Tomorrow was too far away, too long to wait.'

Joanna never moved; in fact, she was incapable of moving. She stood by the towel and simply waited, knowing he would take her in his arms. It was all there in his eyes and her body was already submissive without any command. Her dream was swirling around her and Nick just reached for her, holding her close, his eyes looking into hers.

'You're wet,' she whispered, looking up into his taut face.

'I'm much more than that.' He pulled her tightly to him, letting her feel the hard pulsing desire that held him in its grip, and Joanna wound her arms around his neck and willingly softened against him.

'You feel hot, feverish,' he whispered, his teeth tugging at her ear sensuously. 'You could not sleep?'

'I was dreaming.' Her head fell back languorously, inviting the caress of his lips, and his hands began to move over her slowly, building up the fierce excitement.

'You allow me into these dreams?' he murmured against her ear, his hands stroking her, and she trembled against him.

'I can't keep you out.' Joanna had no sense of self-preservation left. She was too lost, too deeply committed to Nick. If he walked away she would die.

'I won't be kept out,' he whispered. 'I belong there. I want to be there.'

Oh, did he talk to every woman like this? Did he leave what he was doing and fly into the night to be with them? Would she be left with nothing but the dreams? Was that what happened without love?

Joanna gave a soft moan of anguish and his lips captured her, gently forcing her mouth to part, his tongue sliding inside to tease and caress. She was soft, pliant, obedient, surrendering as she had never done before, and Nick groaned against her lips, his hands sweeping over her possessively, finding the swollen evidence of her breasts and lingering to excite them to painful life. She tightened her arms around his neck and moved against him, her hips moving slowly against his, inviting and willing with no real thought of what she was doing.

'What are you wearing?' he asked huskily.

'I never bothered to dress,' she whispered. 'I was dreaming and then—then I had to get out of the house.' She moaned softly. 'I wanted to find you, Nick.'

He gasped harshly and tilted her face, seeing the drowsy submission to desire, her eyes half closed, her lips parted softly, and he crushed her mouth beneath his as his hands swiftly stripped away her nightdress and let it fall to the sand. After years of waiting she was in his grasp, golden in the moonlight, enraptured by desire. He knew she was utterly vulnerable, in need of protection from her own enslavement, but his own passion raged beyond control, burning inside him like a fire.

He ran his hands over her skin, satin-soft, warm and inviting, and his head bent to the pale mounds of her breasts, his tongue flicking against the darkened nipples until she cried out sharply, aching and melting inside. His hands spanned her waist, tightened and slowly moved her from him and she began to whimper softly, struggling to be close.

'Joanna.' His voice was deep and low, and she opened her eyes in bewilderment, shaking her head from side to side, utterly given up to desire. 'I want to look at you.'

He held her trembling body away, his eyes running over her, dark and hungry, moving over every rounded curve, every secret hollow, until she was sobbing under her breath, her legs ready to give way beneath her.

Nick's eyes locked with hers as he pulled her steadily back to him, relishing each second of agony before her skin would meet his, and then his hips were moving against hers, his knee parting her legs, the powerful, thrusting evidence of his need against her soft warmth. They were locked together, as close as in her dreams, and triumph raced through him as she tugged impatiently at the brief black trunks that had been his only covering in the sea.

'Touch me!' He guided her hand between them, groaning as her fingers touched the fierce evidence of his passion, and then he pulled her to the sand, lowering her to the white towel, undressing and moving over her, as irresistible as the waves of the sea, dark, hot power to devour her.

Desire surged through her veins as his dark head bent to her breast, his lips tugging insistently, and she tossed beneath him, her body shuddering with yearning, her mouth too dry to call his name. His hand slid down her body, his palm flat and deliberately heavy, making her gasp as molten feeling surged through her until his fingers slid delicately between her thighs to touch the warm moisture at the very centre of her being.

She cried out then, a sharp cry of ecstasy, and he lifted her into his hips, his feelings now out of control. He knew he must be careful, gentle. His violent jealousy had not blinded him to the fact of her innocence, but she shuddered beneath him, bewitched, eager, intoxicated with desire, and he came into her fiercely, his mouth burning over hers.

Joanna felt the world shatter into a thousand pieces, the brief pain forgotten as the universe exploded around her, stars shooting to a fiery heaven. Pleasure grew to an unbearable pitch as he moved inside her, draining her sweetness until they were both consumed by the flames.

She trembled beneath him as he buried his face in her hair and drew shuddering breath into aching lungs, his heart beating like a hammer above hers. Tears streamed down her face, her body still awash with the vibrant force of feeling, and Nick at last raised his head, his tongue beginning to gather the tears slowly.

He knew what they were, the aftermath of such frenzied desire, and he said nothing, expressed no regret, no joy, his breathing still deep and heavy. He stroked back her hair, his eyes roaming over her face, and then his lips began to bite gently at hers, quick impassioned snatches that became faster and deeper until his arms tightened and she felt the renewed surge of desire race through him.

She felt almost drunk with love, her eyes holding his as he looked down at her, and this time he moved slowly, deliberately, his teeth biting at her gently, his hands stroking her breasts. Pleasure surged through her and she arched against him, her eyes closed as he looked down and watched her face, seeing the enchantment grow as he moved inside her.

'Nick!' She gasped his name and his dark eyes devoured her.

'You need me, *piccola*?' he murmured thickly. 'You need me as I need you?'

She could not answer. She was floating away into the air and this time when she came back she was curled in his arms, his lips trailing over the smooth skin of her shoulder.

'Why did you come back?' she whispered against the strength of his chest and he sighed.

'For this. For you. I was not sure if I could live until morning. You came like the answer to my prayers.' He lifted her face and looked down at her. 'As soon as it is light I must go back. I left in the middle of important negotiations. If I stay here the whole thing will collapse about my ears.'

It was chilling, not what she had expected to hear, although she should have known. Nick was never still, never in one place for very long.

'Where is Charles?' he asked quietly when she said nothing. 'Why does he allow you to roam at night along the beach?'

'He's in Florida. It's to do with the film script.'

'You didn't want to go with him?'

'I'm working. I'm doing free-lance work for Eileen, you know that. In any case, I—I didn't want to go.'

'In case you saw me?' he asked astutely. 'I have not been to Florida for years. You would have been safer there than here. I knew where to find you. I was desperate enough to even come and get you.'

He moved with sudden impatience, pulling on his trunks and standing, lifting her to her feet. 'Get dressed. Your skin is beginning to feel chilled.'

'D-don't watch me.' She was suddenly shy, snatching up the towel and holding it like a shield.

'Why not? You cannot say now that I do not own you.' All the same, he turned away, and Joanna dressed quickly. She was shivering, quite cold and not a little lost. The passion had gone from Nick's eyes, the tenderness had left him as if it had never been there at all, and she knew all over again that she just didn't understand him.

What did he need? What had his strange background left unsatisfied? If she could find the key to unlock his heart she would always be with him, and she wanted that as she had never wanted anything else.

'Are you all right?' Joanna suddenly became aware that she was just standing with bent head and that he was watching her, trying to hear her thoughts.

'Yes. Yes, I'm all right.'

'I hurt you?' His arms lashed around her, holding her close, and he didn't wait for an answer. 'I wanted you terribly and I hurt you. I'm a savage. You have good reason to be scared of me.'

'You're saying that deliberately, working yourself up into a rage for some reason of your own,' Joanna accused, looking up at him, making no move to tear herself out of his arms. She was smiling too, secretly, her mind quite made up. She would fight to keep him, just so much and no more. Even if she had to run away she would leave Nick guessing, wanting her. If she was an obsession that had to burn out then she would keep him guessing for a long time.

'And you are smiling to yourself, smug and satisfied,' he mocked softly. His hand captured her face, holding it fast. 'Come back to New York with me. I want you where I can see you.'

'You don't trust me?' She looked up at him and did some mocking of her own.

'Who can trust a woman?' he muttered, his face slightly puzzled. 'It is not that,' he added impatiently. 'I want you. How long do you think I can live on tonight? It will just make me need you more. You want me tearing back to you each evening until I collapse with exhaustion?'

'Of course not.' Joanna gently extricated herself, smiling into his slightly bemused face. 'For one thing, my father will come back and he'll certainly object. For another, I'm working too. It may not be high-powered and all-consuming, but it's what I do and I enjoy it.'

'What do you mean, working?' Nick exploded. 'You have no need to work. I can buy you the moon.'

'It looks so much better there,' Joanna mused, glancing at the sky. 'As to working, I trained for it. I like it, I'm good at it. *You* may not care for my clothes, but they sell.'

'Who says I do not care for your clothes?' Nick grumbled, picking up his towel angrily. 'You look beautiful with or without clothes. How did we get into this ridiculous conversation? What are you doing to me?'

'Nothing at all.'

'You smug, green-eyed little cat,' he muttered, pulling her back into his arms. 'I want you with me!'

'No, Nick. I'll see you when you get back, but of course my father will be here then.' She knew he would hear the threat and it was very sweet to her; his expression was dumbfounded. Nobody had ever ruled his wild life. She kissed him quickly and then spun away. 'Goodnight, Nick.'

'Joanna!' He caught her in minutes and held her fast. 'I can't live without you.'

'Of course you can. All those women.'

'You don't care about them?' He looked appalled, unbelieving, and she shrugged lightly although jealousy streaked through her at the very mention of them.

'I know all about your life. I've always known. I can't change it and I'm not about to wear myself out trying.'

He was so stunned that he let her walk away, and Joanna almost held her breath. She was taking the greatest chance of her life, challenging him as no one had ever done, and she knew it.

He bounded up the steps as she reached the door.

'Tonight—it was the first time for you. You gave yourself to me more sweetly than any other woman could. It meant nothing to you at all?' His face looked drawn and she smiled into his dark eyes, longing to tell him that even his words just now had made her heart turn over, her tummy clench with remembrance.

'Yes. It meant something to me. I've stopped fighting you.'

'Then come with me, *cara*. Sleep in my arms, be with me.' He began to rain kisses on her face and neck, holding her close. 'We need each other. We set each other on fire. You've moved into my life.'

'We made love, Nick,' she said softly, drawing back to look at him, 'but it doesn't mean I'm one of your women to follow you mindlessly. I have my own things to do, my own life to live. I want to see you again as often as I can, but not as a slave.'

Her hand touched his face gently and then she slipped inside and locked the door. She almost expected to hear him pounding on it, demanding entry, but there was no sound and she knew he was just standing there, something to think about that he had never faced before. Finally she heard him leave. Even his footsteps sounded thoughtful, and Joanna stood with her hand on her pounding heart.

She might have lost him altogether, or she might have opened his eyes to something he had never faced before. She could only wait, wait and hope. She was still awake when she heard the boat leave the island. He was going back; this time he had not used the small plane. He had probably been too tired after his meetings. Had he taken Ed? She hoped so. She wanted him to be guarded, looked after.

She curled up in bed and willed herself to dream because this time she knew the reality; strong arms had held her, passionate lips had kissed her and she belonged to Nick.

CHAPTER TEN

WHEN she saw Nora, Joanna discovered that indeed Nick had taken Colby with him. She tried to get down to work, but at the back of her mind a dread loomed that she had taken a chance that would not come off. Nick had gone away thinking, but what had he thought? Had that one night freed him of his desire? He never rang, in spite of their lovemaking, and once again Joanna's mind turned to the women who still stayed in his life. Maybe she was an oddity and he had dismissed her as such? She could only hope, but it was too late now; in any case, she had made her decision that night on the beach.

Her father came back two days later and he knew something was wrong as soon as he saw her. No amount of smiles could take away the fear at the back of her eyes.

'Are you better, Jo?' he asked when they were alone and settled to their evening drinks on the veranda. 'You look thin, a bit shaken.'

'It was only flu,' she assured him. 'I've been over it for ages, but sometimes things linger.'

'Like Nick. You love him, don't you?'

It needed no real consideration. She had spoken the truth to Nick's grandmother, so how could she lie to her father?

'Yes, I love him. I've gone through all manner of feelings with Nick, from fear to rage, even to simply enjoying his company, but yes, I love him. I can't pretend otherwise and I wouldn't want to pretend.'

171

'And how much more is there?' he asked quietly. 'You're not the same. There's something about you, something deep and different. Are you lovers, Jo?'

'Yes.' She felt no embarrassment, no regrets, because it lingered like beauty in her mind. 'I'm not living with him, I'll never live with him, but we're lovers. He needed me and I needed him.' She stood and walked to the veranda steps, looking out at the brilliant sea. 'He asked me to go with him, but I can't spend my life wondering when he'll tire of me. I couldn't live like that.'

'My poor baby!' Her father came and put his arm tightly round her. 'Do you think he'll marry you?'

'It's not even that,' she said softly. 'I want just one word, one sign. I want to know he loves me.'

'And do you think it's in Nick, to love? I like him, Jo, but I wouldn't want to be a woman in his life. You obsess him. I've known that for some time. I used to think he only made friends with me to be able to get to you, and perhaps my instincts were right. There's a ruthless, driving force in Nick that can't be swept aside. He's a survivor. I can't see him getting married.'

'Or loving?' Jo asked wistfully, looking up into his face.

His expression softened and he kissed her cheek.

'I'm prejudiced. I can't imagine anyone not loving you. Maybe Nick's no exception. Maybe he'll say that one word you're waiting for.'

They didn't talk about it any more, and Joanna spent the evening listening to tales of Florida, exciting words from her father about how he had worked the place into his book. The filming was definite and she was glad to see him happy, although she knew that there was anxiety in him about her.

She lay in bed later without a thought of sleep, her mind on Nick, her own words ringing round in her head.

One word, one sign, that was all she needed, and suddenly she was skimming back in her mind to the fort, to Nick's own words before he had left her with Nora and gone back when she was almost better. She could see his dark eyes looking down at her, hear his voice.

'One word... and you never say it.'

She sat up in bed, staring blindly into the moonlit room. Did Nick need the same word that she herself needed? Did he need to hear the word 'love'? Could it be that he dared not say it in case a confession of that deep kind of need left him lonely once again?

She had tried to play a clever game when in all probability something so gloriously simple had stared her in the face. Many women must have been prepared to give themselves to Nick, some for gain, some because they were simply dazzled. How was he to know that she was different unless she told him, unless she proved it by saying the word?

He was so far away, and perhaps he would not come again. Perhaps he would make a barrier between them to protect himself. She could only wait, praying for another chance. So far the chasing had all come from Nick, and she had run repeatedly. She would never run again, and if she was wrong then at least she would never be sorry.

Nick did not come; days went by and still she never heard the sound she was subconsciously always waiting for. No small bright plane came to circle the island and set down behind the fort. Her father resolutely stayed by her side, reading, walking with her and talking about his work. She worked too, finishing the designs for Nick's grandmother and sending them off to Eileen with a letter asking for urgent action.

One day as she was alone for a while she suddenly remembered about Freddy. After the frantic, tear-filled and selfish call her mother had not been in touch once, neither by letter nor telephone, and Joanna was annoyed when she thought about it.

Not one suspicion entered her mind that Nick would have lied. He had said the bid was withdrawn and it would have been. Nobody knew why, nobody knew that she had been part of it, but any normal mother would have phoned to let her know that the crisis had passed.

Eve was not a normal mother. Joanna had to remind herself of that as soon as she had her mother on the phone.

'Is everything all right?' Joanna asked as Eve came on to the line.

'All right? Of course.'

'So you're not about to be forced into letting Hemmington Manor go?'

'Oh, that?' Her mother gave a short laugh. 'Of course not. I don't know what got into me. The bid was withdrawn and I can well imagine why. Do you remember Mr Martella, Joanna? Martin's wedding, you know? Well, he simply poured money into the business. Frederick is astounded, but delighted, of course. A manager has taken over because naturally Frederick was letting things slip. It all turned out for the best, and so lucky that Mr Martella chose that very time to assist. Nobody would think of standing against him. Unlike Frederick, he's a man you can't challenge.'

Joanna was quietly furious. Her mother really thought of nothing but her own comfort. *Naturally* Frederick was letting things slip, Freddy, who had been so important until she had found a flaw and felt the money slipping away. And did Joanna remember Mr Martella? It was impossible to stand there and chatter. Joanna rang off with a quick goodbye before she was driven to mentioning bootlaces.

She almost told her father when he came in, but of course she couldn't. It was a secret. Telling him would have meant explaining why it had happened in the first place and how Freddy had been saved. Another secret. She couldn't tell him about her little trip to New York to see Nick's grandmother either; that was secret even from Nick.

It was next morning when the plane came in, circling and then sweeping out across the glittering sea, ready to land behind the fort. Joanna heard it from her room. She was not even dressed yet, but at the sound she ran out on to the veranda and watched the small silver bird turn to the island.

'He's come back.' She whispered the words almost to herself, her eyes watching the sky, and her father's arm came round her as he joined her and stood quietly. 'This time I know what to do,' she murmured. 'This time I won't make any mistakes.'

'Oh, love, I want so much for things to go right for you,' her father said softly, but she hardly heard because she was suddenly stiff, frightened, her eyes on the darkening plume of smoke that began to drift from the plane without warning.

'Nick!' She felt her father's arm tighten at the sharp anxiety in her voice and he too watched the sky with dread. The smoke blackened, streaming out behind the plane, a black patch on the blue sky.

Flames followed the smoke and grew in an instant, searing along the silver fuselage like a many-tongued dragon, and the noise came then, the cough of failing engines as the plane lost height and dived towards the sea.

'*Nick!*'

Joanna screamed his name as her eyes opened wildly. The plane hit the water with one wing-tip, turned over crazily, floating for an instant and beginning to sink.

She had no memory of anything else. There was only the sound of her own screaming, her father's frantic attempts to hold her back as she tried to fight clear and race to the sea. Nothing could shield her eyes from the slowly sinking plane, and Nick's name filled her whole being agonisingly.

Rescue boats were there almost at once, fast launches from the bigger island close by, and with them came a doctor, who gave Joanna an injection to loosen the tightly locked muscles and put her to sleep. There was no other way to calm her.

She heard them talking, however, low voices by her door, as the doctor stood with her father.

'They've got one man. He's hurt but safe.'

'Nick?'

She called out as she felt the injection catch hold of her, forcing her voice from some deep woolly cloud, but before they could get into the room she was asleep, unable to fight off the drug. They looked at each other then, exchanging grave glances. It had not been Nick, and Charles Denton walked out to stare blindly at the sea. As long as he lived he would never forget her wild cries as she had called Nick's name. Tears rolled down his cheeks and the doctor poured him a brandy.

'I'll stay,' he offered sombrely. 'She may need another injection.' He poured himself a brandy too. He had never before heard anything like that. She had been in a state of collapse as he had got to the house, and his heart was heavy for the fair-haired girl who still shivered in her sleep. He had not needed to be told who was on that plane and what Nick Martella meant to her. The fact that she had seen it happen was appalling.

* * *

Joanna was kept sedated, and it was not until late in the night that she awoke, and then only partially. The full horror was still held at bay, dulled by drugs, but she knew all the same. She could hear her own desperate weeping, feel her own body shaken by sobbing as she called Nick's name.

Light came into the room as the door opened, and someone sat beside her, taking her hand and holding it tightly.

'Joanna, Joanna, can you hear me, *cara*?'

She knew it was Nick and she also knew it was impossible. Her eyes opened, staring at him blindly, her fingers clutching his.

'Don't go,' she said in a strange, urgent whisper. 'Stay in the dream, Nick. It's all I've got now, and I love you. Stay in the dream, please!'

Her father stood in the doorway, swallowing hard to control racing emotions, but she didn't see him; she clung to Nick's hand, insistently pleading with him in that low, urgent voice. It was chilling, heartbreaking, and Nick bent swiftly, lifting her into his arms and sitting on the bed, cradling her in his lap.

'Wake up!' he ordered fiercely. 'Wake up, Joanna! I'm here. I'm in the room, alive. I was not on the plane. It was Ed and he's all right. I was still in New York, waiting for my flight to Japan. Do you hear me, Joanna? I'm here with you. I'm holding you.'

She looked into his face, trying to fight off the clouds of sedation, struggling to see him more clearly. His face wouldn't seem to keep still and she clasped it between her hands, her eyes dazed, the room swimming.

'Nick?'

'I am here, Joanna. I'm with you.'

His dark head bent and his mouth closed over hers gently, and he stayed like that. Joanna fell asleep with his lips on her own, and after a second he raised his head and looked down into her pale tear-streaked face.

'*Cara, cara mia,*' he said softly.

He put her gently into bed and then walked out on to the veranda, where Charles waited, struggling with feelings so deep that he could not yet control them. Nick's hand came firmly to his shoulder and then he flung himself into a chair and looked up.

'A whisky, Charles,' he said wryly. 'Have one yourself. This has been one hell of a day, and white wine will not do at all.'

They smiled at each other with complete understanding, knowing they would still be there talking and keeping each other company when dawn broke.

When Joanna awoke next morning she was alone. The sound of Nick's voice still seemed to be in her ears, but he was not there. A dream again, only a dream. She put her head in her hands, looking up with unhappy green eyes as the door opened. It was Nick, her father behind him, but she didn't even see her father this time either; her eyes were clinging to the tall, dark man who came towards her.

'Nick!' She stared at him wildly and he pointed one stern brown finger at her.

'No tears,' he ordered vibrantly. 'Not one tear!' He stood by her, his eyes on her dazed face, and then his own face was wreathed in smiles, his eyes softened. 'I am here, *piccola*, alive, well and infuriating.'

'Oh, Nick!' She struggled to get up and he simply lifted her out of bed and into his arms, smiling into her face. She was too filled with incredulity to do anything other than cling to him, her face buried against him, her arms tightly around his neck. 'You're here! You're here!' she whispered.

'Of course I am,' he assured her softly. 'I always have to be. I have no other place to go.'

She looked up at him and his eyes caressed her, roaming over her face adoringly.

'You are still drowsy?' he asked quietly.

'Very. I'll be struggling to stay awake all day.' Her lips were trembling but she couldn't stop smiling.

'I will not,' Nick said firmly. 'I'm going to sleep. Charles and I have been up all night, taking turns to come in and stare at you. We have also, at one time, come pretty close to being drunk. I'm going to bed.' He turned to the door and looked directly at her father. 'I'm taking her with me. If you want her, you know where she is. Come for dinner and bring her some clothes.'

Charles was laughing, actually laughing, when he had never thought to laugh again.

'What about Japan?'

'Where's that again?' Nick turned from the step and grinned at him. 'By now I've forgotten what I was going for.'

He walked off along the beach, carrying Joanna, who curled against him, her slender arm around his neck, and her father watched them, still smiling. Sometimes miracles happened and he thought he was seeing one.

'I saw the plane crash,' Joanna whispered when they were alone, Nick holding her tightly, striding towards the fort.

'I know,' Nick murmured, pulling her closer. 'My office was alerted and I came at once. Another hour and I would have been on my way to Japan. Ed was alone and he was very lucky. He's got a broken arm and a few cracked ribs. They've kept him in hospital.'

'I—I didn't know if you would come back...'

'I had to think,' Nick said quietly. 'You made rules, Joanna.'

'Stupid rules,' she whispered. He never said anything at all and Joanna closed her eyes against the brilliant light. He was here, taking her with him, but he had not made any sort of decision. It was strange, but when she had seen him this morning she had somehow felt that everything was all right.

Last night was still hazy in her mind. She knew he had been there. She knew he was safe, but still dreams mixed with reality because of the after-effects of the tranquillising injections. Was Nick merely being his usual domineering self? She had only hazy ideas as to what her father would think and why he had stood there laughing as Nick had carried her off like some pirate. It didn't matter. He was alive and she was with him.

Nick walked into the house, carrying her, and it was silent, empty.

'Nora is with Ed,' he told her, seeming to be reading her mind. 'She'll be back this afternoon. I can't imagine any hospital holding Ed. He's had cracked ribs before.'

He walked up the stairs and shouldered his way into the beautiful room she had briefly seen before, kicking the door closed and taking her across to place her in the wide, comfortable bed.

'Go back to sleep.'

Nick said nothing more. He simply stood there, peeling off his clothes as Joanna looked up at him in astonishment. She was still too sedated to feel more than a ripple of heated excitement as he stood, golden-brown and naked, and then he slid in beside her, pulling her head to his shoulder, wrapping his arms around her and closing his eyes.

'Nick!' She didn't try to move, but this was so unexpected, almost unreal.

'Later, *piccola*,' he murmured drowsily. 'Right at this moment I am worn out. I know my limitations. In any case, it would be a blow to my ego if you fell asleep as I made love to you.'

He curled her against him firmly as if the matter was quite settled, and Joanna sighed, her lips curving in a smile of sheer contentment because suddenly she knew what she should have known a long time ago: Nick loved her.

It was almost dark when Nick woke her up by tilting her face and placing exotic kisses against her neck. The room was dim, but lights from the patio filtered up to make it possible to see.

'Time to dress for dinner,' he murmured. 'I've just had Nora here. They came back two hours ago. Ed is resting, Nora has the meal ready and she tells me that Phoebe brought your clothes.'

'Nora was in here?' Embarrassment brought Joanna to instant life, her eyes looking frantically around the dimly lit room.

'It's OK,' Nick assured her innocently. 'We whispered. I made sure she didn't wake you.'

'It's not that!' Joanna sat up, looking shocked. 'I—I'm here... What will she think...? I mean...'

'She knows you're my girl,' Nick pointed out, looking surprised as he lay watching her. 'Where else would you be but here?'

'*Nick*!'

He began to laugh and pulled her down into his arms.

'Nobody has been in here. I did my whispering outside the door. When we're married, though, you will have a choice to make. Either Ed comes in with the coffee each morning, or Nora. I can't get out of bed until I've had at least two cups.'

'Married?' Joanna looked at him with so much hope that he hugged her close and kissed her soft lips passionately.

'Married, my darling,' he murmured against her mouth. 'When you were crying for me, begging me to stay in your dream, you told me all I've ever wanted to know, said the words I always wanted to hear. You said "I love you" and those words will keep you in my arms forever because I have loved you since I first saw you.'

He drew back and looked down at her.

'Such a long time, *cara mia*, so long to need you and long for you. You looked at me with fright and then with such distaste. I dared not try to get close to you. And all the time I saw the way your life was going, leading you straight to Martin Sutton. I had to take some action because I could not let you go, and I knew that with him you would be merely a shoulder to lean on. You would still be alone, as I was.'

'Oh, Nick. I didn't love him at all. I was just hiding away from any sort of turmoil, I suppose.'

'So was I,' he said softly. 'I wanted no attachments, no woman to be close to me, but I saw you and it was worth the risk.'

She knew what he meant. One day she would tell him about her trip to see his grandmother, but right now she simply wanted his arms around her. Nick, though, moved swiftly when she melted against him and began to trail her lips over his strong jawline.

He slid down the bed and pulled on a robe that most certainly had not been there before.

'Oh, no, my enticing little cat,' he laughed. 'Very soon your father will be here for dinner and, in any case, I do not intend to be close to you again until after the wedding.'

'Nick!' Her wail of protest had him lifting her into his arms, his smile white and gleaming.

'Well,' he mused, 'perhaps later. If I can convince everyone that you're my girl.'

'Oh, *I* can,' Joanna said happily, wrapping her slender arms around his neck. 'I can convince anyone. Just don't ever be away from me again.'

'Not for a second,' he murmured against her lips. 'Last night Charles and I did a lot of talking. I told you that one day he would give you to me. He did that last night and soon he can do it officially. As soon as we can arrange it.'

They both wanted the wedding to be on Santa Marta, and it seemed to Joanna later that the little white church behind the hill had been filled with celebrities. Nick had flown people out from so many places. Eileen from London, her mother and Freddy, but most of all his grandmother, who had already had a long visit from them when they had flown to New York to see her and tell her their news. She was a warm addition to Joanna's life.

Joanna stood now with Nick on the patio overlooking the sea, and his arm came tightly around her as his dark head bent to hers. All around them the party was still going on, the fort filled to overflowing with guests, but Joanna and Nick seemed to see only each other.

'Oh, darling. I wish they would go,' he whispered against her ear. 'I want you so much, and they will not leave for hours.'

'We'll live through it,' Joanna smiled, turning into his arms and laying her hand along the silken rasp of his cheek. 'This is just one day. We've got forever.'

His arms tightened as his dark eyes devoured her, but the sound of light steps on the patio had them both looking round.

'Oh, Nonna!' Joanna exclaimed. 'You look so wonderful.'

'Thanks to you,' Nick's grandmother said with something like excitement in her voice. 'You were so quick with this design, and they were really fast in London. It came just in time for the wedding. It is slimming, don't you think, and youthful?'

'You look positively girlish,' Nick teased as his grandmother showed off the suit Joanna had designed for her.

'You may laugh,' she informed him firmly, 'but Joanna has too much talent to be kept locked away. I suppose you are going to let her continue to work?'

'If she works from home,' Nick muttered. 'I'm not having her flying back and forth without me.'

'How selfish, Nick. You'll fly back and forth without her,' his grandmother pointed out.

'No.' His voice was very quiet and he shook his head. 'I will never leave her side. In future, things will have to change. I don't belong body and soul to Martella Industries. I belong to Joanna.'

His grandmother smiled as she went back into the room filled with guests. It was no news to her. She had known where Nick's heart lay for a long time, and everything had worked out so wonderfully. Ed Colby came to escort her as he had proudly done all day, and she turned back for one more look at her beloved Nick with his golden bride.

'They look so happy,' she murmured to Ed. 'Just so right together.'

'Yes, ma'am,' he agreed with satisfaction. 'Nick's girl is a real beauty.'

And that was what Nick told Joanna when the place was at last silent and only soft shadows filled the moonlit room above the sea.

'I told you a long time ago that you were mine, darling,' he whispered against her skin. 'I've spent such a long time loving you and waiting for you to love me.'

'Oh, Nick. I was too afraid of your power, too dazzled.
You seemed to offer me emotions I couldn't face. I was
carefully hanging on to the things I knew. I was even
too scared to throw everything aside and go to live with
my father, although I always wanted that. I suppose I
hung on to Martin because of safety. You were danger,
more excitement than I could cope with.'

'You're coping with it very well now, my beautiful
Joanna,' Nick murmured, his lips trailing heated kisses
against her slender neck. He suddenly stopped and
looked down at her. 'Was it wrong to refuse to have
Rina and Martin to the wedding? It was too soon for
me to have him here, but I wouldn't want Rina to feel
hurt.'

'She won't. I've seen to that,' Joanna assured him. 'I
wrote to her and told her all about us. I also promised
a party for the next time they come home. We'll have
another reception, and Rina can bring her lap-dog,' she
added wryly.

Nick grimaced in self-disgust and apology.

'Words, *mia cara*, words to cover my wild jealousy
and my pain. To see you in the arms of another man is
more than I can bear. I thought for one terrible moment
that you would go to him. I could not have carried on
with life.' He sighed and turned her into his arms. 'In
Rina I see my sister, gentle, kind.' He looked at her urgently. 'Do you think he loves her, *cara*?'

'Yes.' Joanna kissed him gently. It was wonderful to
be able to reassure him, to be the warm arms that wel-
comed him. 'He loves her. I know Martin, don't forget.
He's weak and he's a touch selfish, but deep down he's
a very nice person, and from the things he said to me
on the beach I know he loves Rina. All she has to do is
learn to handle him, and she will.'

Nick laughed softly.

'Oh, yes. I know of your visit to Nonna. After a while she could not keep it to herself. She was too filled with joy at the idea of having a beautiful granddaughter, and I think that the thought of clothes specially designed by a rising English designer helped a great deal to provoke the confession.'

'I couldn't tell you until she did,' Joanna protested. 'It was Nonna's secret.'

'She thrives on them,' Nick admitted, 'but eventually she tells me, as you would have done. Neither of my women can keep secrets from me.'

'Neither is a word that suggests two only,' Joanna pointed out, sitting up and looking down at him crossly. 'I'll allow Nonna, but anyone else can just...'

He pulled her down to him, his eyes gleaming with amusement, and for a moment she was being too possessively kissed to speak.

'Let us deal with my women,' he said at last when she was lying breathlessly beneath him. 'There have been women in my life, darling. I was not a boy when I first saw you, but they were brief encounters that meant nothing at all. I was too busy, too occupied with business to give more than a momentary glance at any woman. Since I met you I have probably doubled my travelling time simply to be able to see you, simply to hope that you would be there.'

'You've been seen with women, photographed with them,' Joanna protested.

'As is any well-known person. It does not mean that I then took them back to my apartment.'

'What about that woman in your apartment when I rang you? And what about Céline saying you had been "too busy"?'

'The woman was with her husband. We were going out to dinner, the three of us. As to Céline, I *had* been too busy,' Nick laughed. 'I was not even in New York, and I got a message from the restaurant to say that a man had telephoned for a reservation all the way from England. It had simply invited their close attention, and then he had mentioned my name to be able to get a table. It made them suspicious but it made me race back. I collected Céline and almost bundled her out of her apartment. I prayed that if Charles had a woman with him it would be you, especially as you were obviously determined to escape. That particular vanishing trick did not do much to hide you.'

'No,' Joanna agreed, smiling into his face. 'I was too stunned to be terrified and too angry about Céline to be shy. As you walked in, my heart almost stopped. I should have known then that I loved you.'

'All I care about is that you know now,' he whispered against her lips. 'You are everything I need, everything I desire. I told you I would give up all women for one night with you, and I meant it.'

'Not one night, Nick, darling,' Joanna murmured, melting against him. 'Every night for as long as we live.'

'And even after that,' he promised softly as his lips covered hers and she sank into the deep, warm darkness of love. Now there would be no need to dream. Now it was real and she was safe in Nick's arms forever.

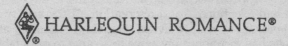

HARLEQUIN ROMANCE®

brings you

More Romances Celebrating Love, Families and Children!

We have a wonderful book for you in April in
our **Kids & Kisses** series—**Bachelor's Family,**
Harlequin Romance #3356, by the ever-popular
Jessica Steele. Fabienne Preston and Vere Tolladine
seem intent on misunderstanding each other until the
two adorable seven-year-old twins, Kitty and John,
play their part in the unfolding romance and make
their dream of being together a reality!

and coming in May...

Harlequin Romance #3362
The Baby Business
by Rebecca Winters

KIDS11-R

HARLEQUIN®

PRESENTS
RELUCTANT BRIDEGROOMS

Two beautiful brides, two unforgettable romances...
two men running for their lives....

My Lady Love, by Paula Marshall, introduces
Charles, Viscount Halstead, who lost his memory
and found himself employed as a stableboy by the
untouchable Nell Tallboys, Countess Malplaquet.
But Nell didn't consider Charles untouchable—
not at all!

Darling Amazon, by Sylvia Andrew, is the story of
a spurious engagement between Julia Marchant
and Hugo, marquess of Rostherne—an engagement
that gets out of hand and just may lead Hugo to
the altar after all!

Enjoy two madcap Regency weddings this May,
wherever Harlequin books are sold.

HARLEQUIN ROMANCE®

brings you

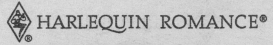

When you read **Invitation to Love** by Leigh Michaels,
you will know there are some wonderful reading hours
ahead of you with our **SEALED WITH A KISS** titles!

In April we have chosen **Dearest Love**, by Betty Neels,
Harlequin Romance #3355, all about sensible
Arabelle Lorimer and the rich and handsome
Dr. Titus Tavener, who both seem to be agreed on
one thing—that they make a very suitable couple.
But what happens when love unexpectedly
enters the picture?

Look out for the next two titles:

Harlequin Romance #3361
Mail Order Bridegroom
by Day Leclaire in May

Harlequin Romance #3366
P.S. I Love You
by Valerie Parv in June

SWAK-2R

HARLEQUIN SUPERROMANCE®

WOMEN WHO DARE
They take chances, make changes
and follow their hearts!

FORBIDDEN
by Ellen James

Having proposed marriage and been turned down flat,
Dana Morgan says to hell with security, her ex-lover and
her old life. Out for adventure, she's prepared for difficulties
and discomfort—and she's eagerly looking forward to the
unpredictable.

What she isn't prepared for is Nick Petrie. Talk about *unpredictable*... And Nick knows it; in fact, he enjoys his reputation.
While Dana tells him to his face that he's a "royal pain," pri-
vately she has to admit he's the handsomest, sexiest, most
exciting man she's ever met. Unfortunately, Nick swears
there's no room in his life for love.

Dana's taking the chance that he's wrong.

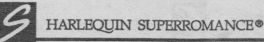

HARLEQUIN SUPERROMANCE®

FAMILY MAN

**He's sexy, he's single...and he's a father!
Can any woman resist?**

First Love, Second Chance
By Amanda Clark

Julia Marshall is leaving New York City and going back to the
Pennsylvania town where she grew up—even if there's not
much to go back for. She'd been raised by cold, unloving foster
parents. And she'd been betrayed by *Tommy Black,* the love of
her teenage years. He'd promised to wait for her, to marry her,
to love her forever. And he hadn't....

Now, ten years later, Tommy's a family man—with a family of
two, consisting of him and his five-year-old daughter, Charlotte,
better known as Chipper. When Julia comes back to town,
Tommy discovers that he'd like nothing better than to make
that a family of three....

Watch for *First Love, Second Chance* in April.
Available wherever Harlequin books are sold.

FM-3